COYOTE
FOR
KEEPS

BURDETTA JOHNSON

COYOTE
FOR
KEEPS

ILLUSTRATED BY JAMES RALPH JOHNSON

A YEARLING BOOK

Published by Dell Publishing Co., Inc.
750 Third Avenue, New York, N.Y. 10017
Published by arrangement with Follett Publishing Company

Printed in U. S. A.
First Dell printing—March 1967

COYOTE
FOR
KEEPS

I

W hat if nobody's there to meet us?"
Marie James's voice sounded scared. Her forehead was pinched, and she stared out the bus
window as if she expected to see her grandfather's
pickup truck bouncing across the rocky desert.

"Grandpa will always be where he says he
will," her brother, Bob, said. "He said in his
letter that he's going to meet the noon bus every
day this week."

Bob gave his sister no clue to his own thoughts. He was a year older than she, and his father had told him that he was in charge on the trip to Arizona.

"But what if Grandma Holmes got sick or something?" Marie whispered. "He'd have to stay with her. Or what if his truck ran into a ditch and he couldn't get out?"

Bob looked at Marie's knuckles on the armrest. They were pale from gripping it so hard.

He looked at her disgustedly. "He could miss us, I guess. He could do almost anything. He won't, though. You're always worrying about something. You've been worrying all spring because you thought we wouldn't get to spend the summer at Grandpa's."

"No, that's not right," Marie answered after a moment. "I've been worrying ever since last fall, when Grandpa first wrote and asked us to come."

Bob tried to hide his own anxiety by keeping his face expressionless. "Look," he said. "Everything's happened just the way it was supposed to. Mother and Daddy said we could go. Uncle Ed picked us up in his trailer truck and brought us all the way from the East Coast to Phoenix. He put us on the bus to Sedona. And when we get there in another hour, Grandpa'll be waiting at the bus station."

"I'd feel better if Uncle Ed had taken us all the way to Grandpa's ranch," said Marie.

"You know why he couldn't do that. His truck could never get up the back road to Grandpa's. Besides, he had to get his truckload to California on time."

Marie said nothing in return. Her face relaxed a little at her brother's show of confidence. The bus windows were partly open, and she turned her nose into the clean pine smell that blew inside from the Mogollon Rim towering above the road to the east and north.

It was an invigorating smell. Bob breathed it in as he studied the rugged slopes, which were still so far away they were more blue than green. Many of the cliffs spotting the slopes were red sandstone, which looked partly purple from this distance.

"Boy, oh boy," Bob breathed after a minute.

"What's the matter?" Marie asked.

"I can hardly wait till we get a chance to explore up in those mountains. I bet they're full of coyotes and deer and a hundred other animals that would make good pets."

Marie looked at him to see if he were serious. "Whoever heard of anyone making a pet out of a coyote?"

"Me," Bob answered.

"A coyote would bite you if you got near it."

"I'm not talking about a grown coyote. I mean a little one that we can raise like a puppy. Most anything you catch when it's little will make a pet."

Marie grinned. "Like that box turtle you picked up last summer and tried to pet. He'd still be holding onto your finger if Daddy hadn't jerked him away."

Bob unconsciously glanced at his little finger even though the turtle had not broken the skin. "He was already grown. If I'd found him when he was a baby, he would have made a fine pet."

Marie continued smiling. "How are you going to catch a little coyote? Chase one down?"

Bob frowned. "Grandpa will know how to catch a coyote if anyone does. He's lived in Arizona all his life."

Marie kept her thoughts to herself for a few moments before speaking again. "I sure wish Mother and Daddy had never moved east. Just think of all the horseback riding and fun they missed."

"Yeah," Bob sighed, in complete agreement with his sister now. "Daddy said he did all that till he went to college. He sure missed out when he decided to live in town."

Bob's gaze drifted to the tall, lean man in the seat across the aisle. He had already studied the man's faded blue jeans, denim shirt, and wide-brimmed straw hat, whose curled brim was soiled from much handling. The three-year-old boy, asleep with his head in the man's lap, was dressed much like his father. Bob wondered what adventures the man and his family had had here in this wooded canyon country. Bob's gaze attracted the man's attention this time, and he turned and smiled.

"I've been hearing you two talking," he said. "I take it this is your first trip out here?"

Marie became suddenly shy upon realizing that their thoughts were not private. Instinctively, she pressed against the seat back. Bob did as he had seen his father do when talking to other people. He answered with a smile.

"That's right. We're going to spend the summer with our grandparents. They run a ranch."

The man nodded and smiled. "You two ought to have a big time. There's a lot of fun for boys and girls around an acre or so of squawling little old calves."

Marie suddenly found her voice. "Acre!" she exclaimed. "Grandpa hasn't got that many calves. He wrote that he's only got three dozen cows in all."

The man's eyebrows lifted, but he grinned kindly. "I thought you meant he raised cattle for a living."

"He does," Marie insisted. "And he's got four little bulls and nine pigs and lots of things like that."

Bob frowned at her in an effort to stop her talking. "That's not what the man means."

"What's your grandpa call his ranch?" asked the man. "I might know him."

"Hardscrabble Spread," Bob answered.

"Hardscrabble?" the man echoed in surprise. "That's a right peculiar name. Folks around here call any place that's too rocky to gallop a horse through, hardscrabble." He shook his head slowly. "Nope, I reckon I don't know your granddad."

As noon approached, the crowded bus got warmer. Bob opened the window as far as he could. Marie sighed, as she had twenty times already.

"I sure hope Grandpa's waiting for us."

"Look," said Bob, turning to her. "Don't you think he's going to make sure he's there or, if he gets held up by car trouble or something, that he's going to have someone there to take care of us?"

"I guess so," Marie admitted.

"Well then, there's nothing to worry about, is there?"

"No." Marie turned back to the window and stared out again at the passing scenery.

It seemed that Bob had hardly gotten the words of reassurance out of his mouth when a strange whistle sounded from directly underneath them. It took another moment for him to realize what it was. With a sickening feeling in the pit of his stomach, he recognized it — a flat tire.

The ancient bus pulled off the road amid a cloud of dust. The unhappy driver shut off the motor before turning toward his passengers.

"We'll be here about twenty minutes or so," he said. "Everybody might just as well get off and take it easy in the shade till I get the wheel changed."

Marie whispered into Bob's ear. "See, what did I tell you? Grandpa won't see a bus. He'll think he missed it and go home."

Bob showed her no sympathy. "You ought to know Grandpa better than that. He'd wait all afternoon if he had to if the bus didn't get there on time."

It seemed that his reassurances were out of luck today, however. By the time they had filed off the bus and found a good vantage spot atop a shady boulder, Bob heard a horn sound.

Looking through the pinyon pines, he saw a bus coming. It was similar to their own. The bus slowed as its driver opened his door and yelled to their own driver, who was already busy jacking up the disabled bus.

"You need any help?" the man called.

"Nope. I'll be through in a few minutes. There's no point in making your passengers uncomfortable by waiting. I'll see you up at Flagstaff tonight."

The new bus picked up speed and ground on out of sight up the canyon road.

"Well, make an excuse now," Marie challenged. "Grandpa will think that's our bus. He won't wait. He'll be back on his ranch by the time we get to the station."

Bob had no ready answer for her now. He tried hard not to show his chagrin. His sister was right. How could he have known there would be two buses today? Now that he thought about it, though, he did remember seeing a lot of people waiting in line behind them when Uncle Ed put them on the bus. The bus company apparently had added another bus to take care of all the passengers.

Bob managed to get in the last word anyhow. "You don't know Grandpa," he insisted to Marie.

2

While they waited for the bus driver to finish changing the tire, Bob's interest shifted to two young Navaho Indian boys. Suddenly one darted from his mother's side to snatch something from the ground.

Bob and Marie sidled close to see what it was. "A horned lizard," Marie said. "Is he lucky!"

The young Navaho exhibited the lizard on his shirt front. The spiny little creature tried to escape at first. But after a few tries, it gave up the attempt as a bad job and settled down on the boy's shirt pocket. Bob and Marie sat down on a rock a few feet away where they could see it easily.

"I bet horned lizards came from dinosaurs," Marie said.

"Are you kidding?" Bob said, glad to see that her thoughts had drifted away from the possibility of missing Grandpa. He decided to use this opportunity to start an argument with Marie; it would keep her mind off their troubles. "A horned lizard is a lizard, and that's all," he said with an emphatic nod of the head.

"It's not much different from an *ankylosaurus*," she commented. "It looks just like one."

"That dinosaur was fifty feet long," Bob stated expertly, knowing very well he was just guessing wildly. He really didn't know how long that dinosaur was — or even if there was one by that name. He had never become so absorbed in the subject as his sister.

Marie looked at him with disgust. "Are you kidding? There never was an *ankylosaurus* over twenty-five feet long." Satisfied with that topper, Marie lapsed into silence.

Bob began to consider a new approach. "Say," he whispered as he nudged her with an elbow, "look at those spines along its back. That boy's going to get stuck yet."

Marie stared at the Navaho boy. He was smiling, for he had been quietly listening to everything that had been said.

"No," the black-haired boy said. "See?"

With one swift hand motion, he dropped the horned lizard into Marie's lap. All the nearby bus passengers turned to watch the expected outburst of fright. Instead, Marie swept up the lizard and held it within inches of her eyes to examine it closely. With her free index finger, she stroked its back gently as if it were a furry animal. To Bob's surprise, the lizard sat quietly like a purring kitten.

"Look at the poor thing," Bob said after a moment, still searching for an argumentative subject. "It's scared."

"It likes the heat from my hand," Marie said as she turned to the Navaho boy.

His disappointment in not getting the frightened scream he had expected seemed to have changed already to admiration. He nodded and grinned.

"That's right. We only see them when it's hot. They crawl under the sand when it gets cold."

"Do they make good pets?" Marie asked.

"No," the Indian boy answered. "They just sit or run away. They most always die if you keep them long."

Marie studied the little horned lizard intently as Bob's attention shifted back to the bus driver. The man was tightening the wheel lug nuts already. In another moment, all the passengers could climb aboard again and be on their way.

Bob's shoulder itched from a twig or something that had blown inside his collar. Before he could scratch it, however, the two Navaho boys broke into a spasm of laughter, and nearby adults began smiling broadly.

Bob looked at Marie. "What's going on?"

Marie's face twisted in a peculiar manner as Bob reached to scratch the persistent itching on his shoulder. Then the truth dawned on him! Lizard feet caused the itching.

The feet slid down the back of his shirt as his frantic hands jerked at the shirttail. The shirttail popped out, but the scrambling feet stayed at his midriff. The undershirt tail!

Bob managed to free his undershirt in the next half second. The horned lizard dropped free and scooted to safety under a boulder.

There was nothing appropriate to say, Bob knew, but he had to say something. "What's the big idea?" he stormed at Marie.

She turned up her hands and shrugged. "I decided not to keep it," she said lightly.

The giggling Navaho boys slapped each other in their merriment, which did nothing to ease

Bob's discomfort. He turned from the boys and scowled at Marie.

The bus driver waved for his passengers now. Bob and Marie joined the line of people returning to their seats. Bob was still stuffing his shirttail in as Marie added a final comment.

"You know, I've decided that a horned lizard *is* different from an *ankylosaurus.*"

Bob and Marie tried to make themselves comfortable in their bus seats again, but it was too hot for any degree of comfort. Unhappy babies and younger children were crying from boredom. Mothers were irritable. Bob wished the trip would end.

The two Navaho boys, their giggling over, were still fascinated with the two eastern children. Their eyes followed every move Bob and Marie made.

Several ranchwomen who apparently had been down to Phoenix on a shopping trip were still full of talk, as they had been the whole trip. Bob guessed they had little chance to visit each other because of their isolated ranches and were making up for lost time.

The friendly rancher and his little boy had returned to the seat opposite Bob. The boy was exhausted from his long trip and waited only until his father had settled before plopping his head into the man's lap again.

A little while later, as the bus rounded a curve, Bob glanced out the window and got his first view of the red rock country of Oak Creek Canyon. His mouth dropped open in amazement.

"Wow!" he breathed.

He had always loved geography and studying about faraway places. As a result, he had seen many pictures of jagged mountains and hidden valleys and other places that hinted of adventure. Here, before his eyes, was a scene that seemed to top them all.

Red sandstone buttes and mesas reared up on all sides for hundreds of feet. The most distant slopes were turned soft blue by growths of junipers and pinyon pines.

The rancher opposite smiled at Bob. "This is some sight when a man first sees it, I guess."

"It sure is," Bob agreed.

"You see that pile of cliffs over there?"

"Yes."

"That's Capital Butte out there across Grasshopper Flat. Its top is over six thousand feet above sea level." The man smiled at Bob's awed interest. "But that big mesa out there is over seven thousand feet. That's Wilson Mountain."

"Some of the names are crazy," Marie said.

The man nodded. "After you've been out here awhile, you'll learn some real odd ones — like Coffee Creek, Little Lo Spring Canyon,

Apache Maid Ranch, Lost Mountain, Secret Canyon, Horse Mesa, and Courthouse Butte." He nodded toward the northwest. "We've even got a Bunker Hill out here, same as they've got out east in Boston. Everything was named for a reason, I guess, but sometimes it's hard to figure it out."

Bob could only imagine the happy days ahead, days of exploring those hidden canyons and rugged mountains. Each was probably well populated with all the western animal life he had studied about for years — bushy-tailed pack rats, kit foxes, jackrabbits, horned lizards, desert white-tailed deer, and, best of all, coyotes.

What an exciting place this must be on a moonlit night, thought Bob. Under a full moon, the mesas probably looked like gold and silver castles. Strange western plants — yuccas, century plants, alligator junipers, ocotillo bushes — would make the scene a wonderland like no other place on earth.

Most exciting of all, though, would be the animals of the night. Owls would sweep past without a sound. Wildcats would stalk kit foxes. The foxes would hunt rabbits. The rabbits would compete with desert tortoises for tender cactus buds. Coyotes would trot to the mesa rimrock, point their noses upward, and let loose long, spine-chilling howls that could be heard for miles. What an exciting chorus that would be!

Of all the western animals, the one that really fascinated Bob was the coyote. It was a wild creature, but still a dog. Bob had read of people capturing coyote pups and taming them. More than anything this summer, he wanted to catch a coyote pup, too, and make it a pet. He knew this would not be an easy job, but, come what may, he would do his best.

Marie interrupted his thoughts. "How far is it to the bus station?"

"How should I know?" Bob answered. "I've never been on this road either."

The rancher across the aisle had some help. "It won't be long now," he assured them. "Another ten minutes and we'll be in town."

Marie brightened. She straightened and tried to see the bus station out the front window, but Sedona was still out of sight beyond the curves and slopes. She put her hand on her stomach.

"Am I ever hungry," she whispered to Bob.

"You can say that again."

"All right. Am I ever hungry."

Bob turned to frown at her, because it seemed he should if he were to take care of his younger sister properly. But it didn't work. Marie had started giggling. Bob kept his face straight as long as he could, then broke into a grin.

"You can chew on Grandpa's letter," he said,

laughing. "That's the only thing I've got that can be chewed up."

They were still giggling a little when the bus slowed down in Sedona. The town was not much more than a few buildings. They were in it before they knew it. Instead of a big city bus station, they found only a sign identifying one of the stores as the place to buy a bus ticket.

Bob had a premonition of trouble as he led his sister off the bus. Although several people were standing around on the sidewalk, he forced himself to concentrate on getting the luggage out of the bus storage compartment for the next few moments. Even as he picked it up, though, he knew that what Marie had been saying was true.

Grandpa was not here.

He must have met the first bus. Since they were not on it, he had left for his ranch.

The people on the sidewalk began drifting away with the bus passengers who had gotten off. The friendly rancher and his little boy disappeared into a small cafe down the street. The two Navaho boys smiled shy good-byes as they looked back before turning around the corner. In another moment, the street was almost deserted.

Bob heard a sniffle at his side. It was Marie. Suddenly she could stand it no longer. She turned her face against his shoulder and sobbed.

"Bob, we've got nowhere to go!"

3

The more Marie sobbed, the less control she had of herself. Her crying shook her shoulders, and she gasped for breath between sobs. None of Bob's shushes or gentle shakes could quiet her.

A pickup truck was parked a few steps away. It had a dog pen built on its bed, and a small sign painted on the side read "Robin Parker, Predator Control." The dogs inside the pen must have heard Marie's sobbing, for suddenly they set up a chorus of howling that eclipsed her crying.

If the moment had not been so serious, Bob would have laughed at the dogs trying to out-howl their human competitor. However, he had the same frantic feeling Marie had, and he knew he didn't dare let her sense it. She would really go to pieces then. He tried to force his thoughts to be calm. "Think this out," he told himself. "There's got to be something we can do."

They could not set out walking toward the ranch. It was probably miles away. Besides, he really had no idea where it was.

They could wait right here until tomorrow afternoon. But that would be silly, and humiliating, too, when people started closing their stores and turning out lights. They would ask questions that he couldn't answer. They would want to know why his grandpa had not met him and Marie, and they would get mad at Grandpa, when it really was not his fault.

The dogs were still howling when Bob's thoughts were interrupted by a voice asking, "Say, what's the matter, young lady?"

Bob turned to see a grizzled, rawboned man who looked as if he had lived outdoors most of his life. He apparently was the dogs' owner, Robin Parker.

"Well," Bob answered, "someone was supposed to meet us here at the bus station. He just hasn't got here yet, and my sister's scared."

Hearing this, Mr. Parker frowned a little, his forehead wrinkling. But as Marie's crying slowed, and she wiped her tears away with the back of one hand, he smiled.

"You don't have anything to worry about, little lady," he said. "We'll get you two kids to where you're going."

Marie burst out in a final fit of sobbing. "But we don't know where we're going!" she wailed.

"Now, now," soothed Mr. Parker as he sat down on his heels before Marie. "We'll find out."

"She's right," Bob said. "We're going to visit our Grandpa and Grandma Holmes, but we don't know where their ranch is. We've never been there before."

"Holmes," Mr. Parker said to himself. "I know some of the ranchers up in this part of the country, but I haven't run across them yet. I haven't been here too long myself, though."

Bob's gaze swept over the man's thick-soled cowboy boots. The cowhide over the toes was so badly scuffed and scraped that Bob could not be sure if the boots were black or brown.

"I just come around these parts when I'm hunting coyotes or bobcats," Mr. Parker explained as he stood up. "You two stay put, and

I'll look around a store or two to see who knows your grandpa and grandma and how we can get in touch with them."

Mr. Parker had just turned toward the little cafe a few doors down the street when Bob saw an older man step out of the cafe door. The man glanced in their direction, stopped short in surprise, then broke into a jog up the sidewalk.

"Grandpa!" Marie squealed. She dropped her small handbag and raced toward him.

Mr. Parker paused, and his mouth spread in a grin. "Now, how about that?" he said as he turned toward his truck.

Grandpa, with Marie caught up in his arms, soon reached Bob. Freeing one arm from Marie, he gave Bob a quick hug.

"I guess I threw a scare into you two young 'uns," he said, shaking his head. "I found out from the first bus driver that another bus would be along in a little while, so I figured I had time for a cup of coffee."

He let Marie slide to the ground, but she kept a tight grip on his hand. Now that she finally had him, she would make sure that he did not get away. Grandpa picked up most of the luggage, and Bob followed him to his dusty pickup truck a few yards away.

"You know," Grandpa said as Bob opened the truck door, "I bet I know two thirsty young 'uns after that bus ride. How about some good cold orangeade — and hamburgers?''

In a few minutes, Bob and Marie were busy pulling the delicious icy drink through soda straws. Each drank two bottles before the hamburgers were off the griddle.

Before long, Grandpa's pickup truck was out of town and winding along a canyon road toward higher country. Bob remembered his writing once that the ranch was a mile high in elevation.

"I can hardly wait till we get there," Marie said as they bounced along with dust boiling behind. "I'm going to kiss Grandma Holmes, and then stand out back and yell as loud as I can, and throw rocks till I'm tired."

This tickled her grandfather. "That'll make the gophers and grasshoppers sit up and take notice," he said, laughing. "They'll have to move over and give you city folks stretching room."

"Say, Grandpa," said Bob, "do you think we can find some pets this summer?"

"Could be. Could be," answered Grandpa. "The ranch isn't very pert this year, though. Fact is, it's right peaked looking."

Bob looked at him to see what he meant, but Grandpa was staring off across a flat where the grass was dry and sparse. Bare ground showed in many places as if this part of the state were little more than a desert.

"It looks kind of dry," Marie ventured.

"That's what I mean," Grandpa said.

"Doesn't it ever rain?" Marie asked.

"Yes, it does," Grandpa said. "We've had about as much rain this year as we ever did. That's not the reason we're so dry. But anyhow, you might find some pets, and you might not. This dry weather has made wild animals kind of scarce."

As they bounced along, Bob gazed happily past Marie at his grandfather. There were no other grandpas like his own, Bob decided. A perpetual twinkle seemed a part of Grandpa's eyes, and he always found the bright side of any situation. There was something worth laughing at in almost every happening, Grandpa had told him once.

The real reason everyone liked Grandpa so much, Bob thought, was that he could laugh at himself. Bob's father had told him once about Grandpa having to walk fourteen miles to get home one night after his horse threw him. Grandpa thought it was a joke on himself — not being able to stay on a horse after being raised in the saddle.

Grandpa roared every time he told about going fishing in Mormon Lake one summer when he was a boy. He had caught a nice mess of fish, put them in a paper bag, and then laid his shirt and pants on them while he went swimming. While he was in the water, a mountain lion smelled the fish, snatched them up, clothes and all, and bounded away. Grandpa had to walk several miles back to camp in just his underwear.

"How far to the ranch now, Grandpa?" Bob soon asked. He could not hold back his impatience as each turn of the wheels brought him closer and closer to the happiest summer he could imagine.

"Not far," Grandpa answered with a grin. "Just around a few more rocks and bushes."

"What do you suppose Grandma Holmes is doing right now?" Marie asked.

"Well, she's probably got supper headed for the cookstove while she keeps one eye aimed out the front door to see if I'm going to bring back anybody except myself. And she's probably whistling to herself without knowing it and stirring around with a broom in one hand and a pan of cinnamon rolls in the other and . . ."

"Really?" Marie asked.

Grandpa chuckled. "Well, no, not really, but the next thing to it. I think she's just about as eager to see you two as you are to see her."

The pickup truck turned into a wide canyon that wound back into the high mesa country. Bob saw the ranch house sitting a half mile ahead. Its roof was shaded by sycamore trees, and the line of cottonwoods behind the house marked the course of the creek that drained the canyon. The countless tufts of white that floated in the air like summer snow were the fluffy seeds of these cottonwood poplars.

Even at this distance, Bob could see Grandma Holmes step out onto the front porch as she dried her hands on her apron. She waved, and shortly the pickup rolled to a stop in front of her.

Marie was first out, scrambling over Bob's lap in her eagerness. Her happy shout voiced Bob's own thoughts.

"We're here, Grandma Holmes! We're here!"

4

Bob's eyes and ears were alert to many new sights and sounds this first evening at the ranch. As he helped his grandfather stack stovewood on the back porch, he glanced up at the rimrock to the east several times.

This rim of the mesa caught the last rays of the sun long after the canyon had darkened. It changed color every few minutes — from yellowgold, to red, to pink, to purple. When the sun finally dropped below the horizon, the rimrock turned pale blue, reflecting the cool light of a full moon.

This sight, however, was not the main feature. It was only the background for the sounds of a western night. First came the sound of dogs barking, short sounds that grew louder and melted together into a long howl.

"Whose dogs are those?" Bob asked.

" 'Those dogs' are really one animal, one that belongs to the Indians. They figure he was the critter that brought sunlight to the earth."

"What?" asked Bob.

"That's your coyote you've been talking about. Some of the Indians thought he was something to bow down to."

"Are you kidding?"

"No, I'm not kidding," Grandpa answered. "They thought the coyote was so smart that he had to be something straight out of the sky." Grandpa pointed up to the rim where the barking originated. "Before long, another one or two will show up. Just wait a minute."

He hardly had said this when another coyote repeated the howl. Before it was well started, another, and then a third, joined the wild chorus.

Bob had often wondered just how a coyote would really sound. Now he knew. He didn't know whether he liked it or not, but there was one thing sure. The howls sent chills up and down his spine.

Marie stepped out of the kitchen, the dish towel still in her hands.

"Is that really a real coyote?" she asked her grandfather, although she had heard his remarks to Bob.

"As real as they come."

"Do they get up there and howl every night?"

"Not on that particular spot. They're too smart to use the same spot every night. But each little bunch has some favorite howling places, and maybe once a week they'll use the same spot."

"Why do they move around?" Marie asked.

"Probably to keep folks with rifles from knowing too much about what they're doing."

"How far away do you suppose they are, Grandpa?" Bob asked.

"Oh, about a half mile, I guess. Usually you can hear them a mile or so." Grandpa began brushing the stovewood bark off his clothes before washing for supper. He stopped and pointed up canyon. "Some nights when the air is just right — kind of in layers because of different temperatures — you can hear the coyotes for several miles. The noise bounces off the air layers as if they were ceilings in houses."

Marie cocked her head to one side. "I think I hear some more coyotes way off that way." She pointed to the hills in the west, which showed black against the moonlit sky.

"I can't hear them," Grandpa said, "but you two kids've got better hearing than I do. Before long, you'll probably hear them in several directions."

"They sound just like they're talking to each other," Marie said.

"They are," Grandpa confirmed. "Sometimes when one coyote's got something on his mind — like a pack of greyhounds down below him — he'll send up a howl to tell his buddies. In a few minutes, the news may spread twenty miles."

"From the sound of that howling," Bob remarked, "there must be a dozen up in that one spot."

"Not quite," Grandpa said. "Before one has finished, another begins. Three can sound like fifty."

Whatever the number, Bob thought, they certainly made this place seem wild and exposed. Just now he would not be surprised to see an Apache slipping around the barn or a buffalo trotting across the backyard. The coyotes seemed to be able to reach into the past, pull out the excitement and adventure of frontier days, and play the background sounds all over again. They were just like wilderness record players playing the natural music of this wide open country over and over again.

To have a coyote pup for a pet would be almost like holding a little bit of the past, a past still living in the present. Roads and bridges and towns had changed the looks of the land, thought Bob as he sat down at the supper table, but the coyotes had not changed since the days of Coronado, Kit Carson, or Billy the Kid.

Bob's thoughts snapped back to the present when Grandma Holmes began lifting lids off the cooking dishes. Crisp fried chicken filled one platter; a half dozen drumsticks stuck out of the golden pile of crunchy goodness. Hot mashed potatoes steamed in the cool evening air. Bob soon had an adequate mound on his plate, which he decorated with a butter chunk. The butter changed into yellow lava flowing down the potato volcano's sides.

Then Grandpa lifted the napkin over the Indian basket full of biscuits. "Who wants green biscuits?" he asked with a poker face.

"Green biscuits?" Marie gasped. "Whoever heard of green biscuits?"

"All right, then. No green biscuits for you." Grandpa smiled as he fished out one that was a delicate pink.

Marie's mouth was still open in surprise as Grandpa asked Bob, "What color for you?"

Grinning broadly, Bob tried to think of a color that probably was not in the basket. "Blue," he said.

"How about some right nice turquoise, just the color of the Navahos' beads?"

It was true. Bob opened the hot biscuit to find its interior the soft blue color of the turquoise Indian jewelry he had seen. Marie was already nibbling hers.

"Why," she exclaimed after a moment, "it tastes just like any biscuit!"

Grandma Holmes's face had been one big smile since she had sat down.

"That's good," she said. "It had better taste like any biscuit. That's just food coloring in it. We have colored biscuits on special occasions."

"What kind of special occasions?" Marie asked.

"Oh," Grandma Holmes answered, "like when grandchildren come to see us mostly."

Bob couldn't remember when a meal had tasted so delicious. The cool air here, so high above sea level, really built an appetite. He managed to try one of every color in the biscuit basket, and the little volcano of mashed potatoes soon disappeared under the steady digging of his fork.

"I know two kids who'll have a hard time sleeping tonight because they're stuffed," Grandma Holmes said as they finished eating.

"Hey, you mean we get no dessert?" Grandpa asked.

"Well, if anybody's got room left . . ." Grandma Holmes stepped to the wooden cupboard near the back door and lifted a cake from its shelves.

"Wow!" said Bob. "My favorite." He frowned at the trap in which he had placed himself by not saving room for dessert. "Are you going to cut it now, Grandma Holmes?"

"I suppose I ought to look inside and see if it's the right color and everything."

Bob's eyes followed the knife blade as it sank through white icing and emerged with a coating of chocolate crumbs.

"Devil's food," he whispered. "Boy, oh boy."

Bob and Marie managed to make one-inch slices disappear, and when Grandpa suggested they help Grandma Holmes with the dishes before they all took a walk down to the mailbox, Bob had no complaints. He appreciated the chance to work off the huge meal.

As Marie cleaned the table for Grandma Holmes, who was washing the dishes, Bob and Grandpa pumped the back porch water barrel full again. Then they dried the dishes.

The kitchen furniture fascinated Bob. It all appeared to be handmade and very old.

"Did you make these cabinets, Grandpa?" he asked.

"Yep. Your grandmother and I rode into this canyon on a wagon before anybody else lived around here much. We put up in an old miner's cabin down by the creek till we got the house up. Then we sawed out our own lumber and made everything board by board. It didn't come out very fancy, but it didn't cost much either."

"Did anyone ever find any gold or silver around here?" Marie asked.

"Well, yes, I guess they did at one time or another. I never wasted time looking for any, though."

"Didn't you ever want to be rich?" Bob asked.

"Well," Grandpa said, "I think that's what most folks would like to be." He sidled over to Grandma Holmes, who was finishing up at her dishpan. Giving her skirt a playful tug, he smiled and said, "This old girl you call Grandma, and her husband, are right rich."

Bob looked at him with questioning eyes.

"We've got a lot more than all those folks down in Phoenix and Tucson. We've got all the fresh air we need. We've got nice cool summers that are air conditioned inside and outside the house. We've got plenty of room to yell out the back door the way you wanted to, and we can throw rocks at the cows if they poke their heads through the wrong fence. We've even got the biggest bathtub you can shake a stick at — a pond in the creek."

He was thoughtful for a moment before adding, "Come to think about it, we've got so many things to do and see we don't have time to accumulate much money."

The walk to the mailbox confirmed Bob's notions about the wonders of a western night. Even after he went to bed, he was too full of the sounds and smells and sights to go to sleep easily. Everything continued to fascinate him.

The night sounds were just as he imagined they would be. From down canyon came a distant hooting that resembled the calls of the eastern whippoorwill.

"What kind of bird is that?" Marie whispered from her bunk on the other side of the room.

"It must be a poorwill," Bob replied. "I've never heard one before, but they're supposed to be about like whippoorwills."

"I don't like it. It sounds scary." Marie's whisper was muffled.

Bob glanced toward her bed. Enough moonlight came through the window to reveal the bed covers pulled over her head. Bob started to say something about it. Then he realized he had his own bedspread pulled tight around the back of his head. Only his eyes and nose stuck out, like a woodchuck's from its hole.

The night offered a good snuggling temperature. It was cool enough for blankets, and the feather mattress fluffed up all around Bob's sides. Its mustiness was pleasing.

From somewhere in the walls, a cricket chirped with the regularity of a clock. Several toads down in the creek croaked as steadily. The coyotes kept up their periodic yodeling. Overhead, on the roof, the scurrying of rodent feet told of exploring flying squirrels or pack rats.

Bob had never seen a pack rat, but he remembered now about one of Grandpa's letters last year, which mentioned the little animals.

"We've got a big family again," Grandpa had written. "Among other things, a passel of bushy-tailed pack rats live close by and come and visit pretty often. They've made themselves at home, and they've got a bad habit of changing things around every once in a while."

This was the first time Bob had thought about pack rats since then. He had never quite understood what Grandpa had meant by their "changing things around." He guessed Grandpa meant that they changed their nests from place to place.

5

At dawn, Bob awoke to the sound of a faint drumming upon the floorboards. He was still sleepy, for the long trip by truck and bus had exhausted him. Consequently, his eyes saw the little animal on the floor, but his mind refused to function so early.

The animal looked like a small buff-colored squirrel. However, its bushy tail was not as fluffy as a squirrel's. Its chest was snow-white. It thumped the floor with one of its hind legs in a movement so fast that the leg was only a blur, and it held its tail next to the floor like a rigid feather.

As Bob lifted his head in rising curiosity, the little animal scurried out of sight. Bob decided it was not worth the trouble of chasing it. Grandpa could tell him what it was later.

A short time later, Bob was awakened abruptly by a feather pillow smashing him in the face. Raising himself to his elbows, he stared at Marie. She was standing before him getting ready to swing the pillow again.

"What's the matter with you?" Bob yelped, jerking his feet up to catch the impact.

"What did you do with my shoes?" she demanded.

Bob relaxed against his own pillow again. "Well, since I wear them so often, I wore them to bed in case I walked in my sleep."

"That's not funny. Hurry up and get them. Grandma Holmes wants me to help her get breakfast." She threatened him with the pillow again.

Bob grabbed his own pillow to defend himself. That started the action, and in another moment, the two were flailing each other with the huge feather cushions. Grandma Holmes stopped it when she stuck her head in the door.

"Hey, you two. You'll tear up my pillows."

"He hid my shoes, Grandma Holmes." Marie pointed beneath her wooden bunk. There were no shoes there, but an old marble and a snail shell were resting where the shoes had been.

"I did not," Bob answered as he pulled a feather from his mouth. "What would I want with her shoes?"

Grandma Holmes began laughing. After a moment, she looked over her shoulder.

"Come here, Grandpa," she called. "Marie's shoes walked away."

Grandpa came in from the kitchen. He was grinning. "It looks as if the collectors have been at it again," he said.

Puzzled, Bob watched his grandfather step to the closet door, which was made of roughly-sawn lumber. Grandpa opened the sliding door wide and bent to the closet floor. As Bob and Marie leaned over his shoulder to see, he lifted up a loose floorboard.

"That's what I thought." Grandpa chuckled. "Look."

In the dim light below the floor, Bob spotted one of Marie's red shoes. It was wedged between two boards. Grandpa retrieved it, then felt around under the floor another moment before finding the other one.

"Who did that?" Marie asked.

"The collectors," answered Grandpa with

a smile. "The bushy-tailed pack rats. They tried to move your shoes out to their nest in the cactus clump near the barn." Grandpa pointed to the marble and the shell. "They only traded. Most of the time they leave some special treasure for what they've taken."

Marie examined her shoes and satisfied herself that no damage was done. Then she slipped them onto her feet.

"What in the world would they want with my shoes?" she asked. "They can't wear them or eat them."

"They liked their color most likely and wanted to use them as decoration," said Grandpa. "They'll haul anything off to their nests."

Grandma Holmes nodded toward the kitchen. "They like anything bright, especially if it's shiny," she said. "Somewhere down there in the cactus are three forks, a table knife, five teaspoons, an egg beater, and such things as a little glass salt shaker, all kinds of loose buttons, and even a bottle of aspirin."

"Can't you just stop up all the cracks in the house and keep them out?" Marie asked as they all went into the kitchen.

"I've tried that," Grandpa said. "They just gnaw new cracks when I stop up the old ones."

"What about using a big tomcat to catch them?" Bob asked.

"We've got one — old Big Bill, who spends most of his time out around the barn. I can't get him to sit still under the house long enough to make much of a dent in the pack rat population." Grandpa clucked his tongue. "To tell you the truth, I'd hate to see Big Bill catch all the pack rats."

"Why's that?" Marie asked.

"The pack rats gather our pinyon nuts for us each fall. They pick them up in October on the pine slope above the house here. They put them in their nests, which are nothing but big piles of grass and cactus pads. The cactus keeps most animals from bothering the nests, but I use a pitchfork to lift off the top to get to the nuts. I usually get a bucketful each week for a month or so every fall."

Marie was concerned. "Won't they starve to death in the winter then?"

"Not those little rascals," Grandpa said. "They're like honeybees. They fill their storehouse right back up again as if it had never been touched. They keep doing it until the pinyons are gone; then they start using acorns."

Bob smiled. "And that's when you stop emptying their nests?"

Grandpa grinned and nodded.

During breakfast, Bob's thoughts turned to the day ahead. "Grandpa, can we go anywhere we want to around the ranch and do whatever we want to?" he asked.

Grandpa finished his mouthful of pancake before answering. "Well, I guess so. After breakfast, I'll show you around a little and tell you what to stay out of. Then if your grandmother doesn't want any help, you can spend most of the day on your own."

Grandma Holmes had no immediate chores, and shortly the three stepped off the back porch into the warming sunlight.

"Grandpa, is there a swimming hole in the creek?" Bob asked.

"Well, kind of a swimming hole — if you're small enough."

Bob and Marie followed their grandfather a short distance across a field of dried grass and cactus. They headed toward a line of cottonwood poplars, which marked the nearby creek's course.

"There's not much water down there now because the creek nearly dries up every summer these days," said Grandpa.

"Don't you have as much rain as you used to?" Bob asked as they detoured around cactus clumps.

"Yes, we do," answered Grandpa, frowning. "A lot of people, though, would like to think the range has dried up because of not much rain."

"Well, what other reason is there for things

not to be nice and green?" asked Marie as she stepped on a crisp mullein plant. Its velvet green leaves were already dry and brown around the edges.

Grandpa shook his head. He paused to pull the dry seed stalk of a weed from the ground.

"It takes a few years for folks to find out what the big secret is — even if they've lived around here all their lives."

He stripped the few seeds off the stalk as they continued toward the creek. Holding out his hand, he showed Bob and Marie the several seeds in his palm.

"Each year's seeds get eaten up mostly by rats. Just about all the grass seeds wind up in a rat's stomach and never get a chance to grow. Before you know it, you've got no grass to speak of, and the ground dries out, and the water table sinks lower."

Bob thought a moment. "Well then," he said, "why doesn't somebody get rid of the rats?"

"That's what folks are coming around to thinking now. But getting rid of them is easier said than done."

"How did people use to get rid of rats out here?" Marie asked.

Grandpa explained, "Well, they're just now getting around to remembering how the Indians and the first ranchers out here got rid of them."

There were no more questions for the moment. Bob spotted a movement among the cottonwood trunks and broke into a run, with Marie at his heels. The movement was made by a white wading bird, which flapped into the air and headed down canyon.

"A snowy egret!" Marie exclaimed. She turned to her grandfather. "I didn't know you had those out here. I thought they just lived in our part of the country."

"They make themselves at home here, too," Grandpa said, "especially now that the creek is low. Minnows and bigger fish get trapped in potholes, and the fish-eating birds have a picnic."

Bob looked at the green pond formed by the creek. It was not very wide — about six good steps. It was twice as long, however.

"Is it all right to go wading, Grandpa?" he asked.

"I think so. Roll your pants up over your knees. I don't think you'll find a spot more than knee deep."

Bob and Marie wasted no time taking off their shoes and wading into the cool water. The pond bottom was soft sand with no sharp rocks to disrupt its comfort. Bob led Marie in explorations along the pond's length and found the deepest part hardly knee-high. Downstream the water disappeared into a gravel bank. It reappeared many yards farther as a series of small potholes in the flat sandstone that bedded the creek.

Their grandfather waited patiently until they had had their fill of wading. Then he helped them dry their feet, using his huge handkerchief as a towel. As she tied her shoes, Marie glanced up toward the rimrock across the creek.

"Will it be all right for us to go up there by ourselves, Grandpa?" she asked.

"I think so. Just be sure that wherever you go around here, you stop every little piece and look back the way you've come so you'll recognize it when you get ready to go back." He looked at the horizon around him. "I want you two to make sure you always let me or your grandma know where you're going and when you'll be back every time you step out of the yard."

Bob and Marie nodded that they would comply. As they started back across the dry field toward the barn, Marie remembered a question. "Say, Grandpa, what was the Indian secret?"

"What secret?"

"About getting rid of the rats."

Grandpa laughed. "Oh, the Indians just left alone the things that ate the rats — hawks and foxes and bobcats and, most of all, coyotes."

"Well, if it's that easy," Bob said, "how come people don't leave them alone now?"

"Most ranchers — knowledgeable ones, that is

— do just that. But years ago the state and stock associations got to paying bounties on bobcats and coyotes because the sheep raisers lost some of their stock to them. Then some folks started making their livings off killing coyotes and other predators for the bounty payments."

"I guess the ranchers who raise sheep are happier anyway," Marie suggested.

"Not as happy as they thought they'd be," said Grandpa. "The sheep have less grass to eat. The range won't support as many sheep now as it did when the coyotes were thick."

Bob was silent for a moment as they walked along. Then he spoke up. "Why don't we do something about it, Grandpa?"

"What do you have in mind?"

"Raising coyotes."

Grandpa laughed aloud. "Well, I hadn't given much thought to that. I'm afraid it would take a right smart bunch of coyotes to make a real dent in the rat and ground squirrel population now."

6

Their path across the field took them past a small herd of white-faced Hereford cattle standing beneath some trees. The animals stood motionless except for their lower jaws, which were busy chewing their cuds. It was a curious process to Bob. He remembered studying in science about this peculiar ability of certain hoofed animals to ruminate, or rechew food already eaten.

"You sure have a lot of cattle, Grandpa,"

Marie commented as they passed the cows.

"Well, they're not really mine. They're just boarding out here."

"You mean you're a cattle rustler?" Bob said with a laugh.

"Not quite," answered Grandpa, chuckling. "When the big ranchers check their cattle before shipping them to market, they send off the fat ones and hold the skinny ones for special feeding so they'll fatten out, too."

"Then you're making these fat for somebody else?" Bob asked.

"Yep. I'll keep these for a few weeks on my little place here. Then I'll board out some other rancher's stock. I can do it for a living because my ranch doesn't take much to run. But the big ranchers would lose money piddling with a few cows that need special attention. I've got just enough land to raise the alfalfa and corn I need."

Marie gazed at her grandfather in admiration. "You must be awful smart, Grandpa, to know how to do things like that. We don't ever learn things like that in school."

This tickled Grandpa and he laughed aloud. "They didn't show me too much about it in school either," he cackled. "A fellow just picks up the information here and there and learns from his mistakes and runs across a few secrets."

"What are some of your secrets?" Marie asked after a moment.

Grandpa was silent for a few steps before answering. "Well, one is that haystack over there."

Bob followed his gaze. The haystack was an ordinary one, with nothing special about it as far as he could tell.

"That's one way I've got of watering my fields," Grandpa said. "I'm a dry farmer, as folks here call a farmer who doesn't irrigate. That hay there is alfalfa."

"Are you joking about that stuff watering your fields?" Marie asked suspiciously.

"No," Grandpa answered. "It's like this. That alfalfa has roots that reach down into the ground many, many feet farther than the roots of other crops. Those long roots break up the hard ground, and when they die, each root leaves a little tunnel. Then when it rains, instead of most of the water running off to the creek, a lot of it goes down those tunnels, and the ground soaks it up like a sponge. Then when I grow corn for the next crop, the ground is as moist as it should be."

"How about that!" Bob exclaimed. His respect for a grandfather who seemed to have an endless store of special knowledge was no less than Marie's.

Near the barn, Grandpa pointed to a track in the dust.

"Can you guess what made that, Bob?" he asked. Each footprint showed four toes with a distinct claw mark at the front of each toe.

"It looks like a dog's track. I didn't know you had a dog."

"I don't. That was made by Mr. Coyote himself last night. He probably was figuring on stealing one of your grandmother's chickens again. She's not very happy about such visits."

Bob studied the track more closely. He tried to find some difference between it and a dog track, but he could detect none. Nevertheless, he was excited to know that a coyote would come so close. It made having a pet coyote more of a possibility than ever before.

After Grandpa finished showing Bob and Marie the barnyard and other features of the little canyon ranch, they all headed toward the house.

"I'm hungry," Grandpa said.

"Me, too," said Bob and Marie at the same time.

Grandma Holmes met them at the back porch. A frown wrinkled her face.

"The pump's broken," she said.

Grandpa shook his head. "Uh, oh. I was afraid of that. I'll see if I can fix it after we eat."

After lunch, he began the tedious job of taking the pump apart. He continued his work into the afternoon as Bob and Marie helped their grandmother in the kitchen.

"How about our getting a bucketful of wild plums for a pie and some jelly?" Grandma Holmes suggested to Bob and Marie.

She had no trouble getting suitable enthusiasm from the two. So, while Grandpa worked on the pump, they walked down to the mailbox on the main road, and Grandma Holmes led them to a nearby thicket of wild plum bushes.

Gathering the fruit was fun. Everything about this life in the open western country suited Bob. His interest in seeing more sights grew each time he looked toward the rimrock that topped the canyon walls on either side.

"Do you ever go up on the mesa, Grandma Holmes?" he asked when they had finished filling three tin pails with the soft plums.

"Well, your grandfather and I used to walk up there sometimes on Sunday afternoons to look around. We haven't been up there lately, though, because I'm not as much of a mountain climber as I used to be."

"Can we go up there in the morning, maybe?"

"I don't see why not, if your grandfather doesn't need any help."

They walked back along the road toward the

ranch house. Grandpa was still working on the pump when they got back.

"I'm going to have to go into town in the morning and get some parts at the hardware store," he said. "It's too late to go today before the store closes."

That night Bob lay awake for an hour listening to the coyotes howling in the distance. Each wild cry increased his desire to get one for a pet.

At the breakfast table the next morning, Grandpa asked, "Who wants to go to town with me today?"

Both Bob and Marie shook their heads.

Bob asked, "Do you care if we go up on the mesa while you're gone?"

"I guess not, as long as you don't wander off into the next county."

By the time Grandpa was in his pickup truck, Bob and Marie had crossed the creek and were climbing the slope toward a gully that cut through the rimrock. It provided an entrance to the mesa. As they neared the top, Bob could see the dust raised by the pickup, which was now a mile down the canyon.

The mesa seemed like a new world. There were no canyon walls here to make a fence. Bob could see for miles in all directions.

Grandpa's pickup was out of sight now, but another vehicle was coming up the road in the distance. Bob could not see it clearly, though something at the back of his mind suggested that he had seen it before.

Although Bob had never had much of an interest in plants, the new varieties here caught his attention as he and Marie explored through the rocks and low bushes. He looked to see which plants might have been nibbled by a mule deer or an antelope, and which could conceal a coyote or a bobcat.

Patches of red beardtongue flowers stood up among the rocks. Each stalk held several dozen tiny trumpet-shaped blossoms, which caught the sunlight and turned it into sparkles.

What appeared to be fluffy red bird feathers tucked among the rocks turned out to be the flowers of the fairy duster, a plant that made a fairyland of color wherever it grew.

There were also large growths of still another red plant, the Indian paintbrush. Its flowers were practically invisible, but its upper leaves made up for the lack. They were a brilliant scarlet and as soft and velvety as a chick. Bob imagined that coyotes would love to romp through these lush plants, not only to uncover rabbits and rodents, but to feel the gentle brushing of the plants against their stomachs.

Their quiet explorations among the rocks and plants continued as Bob led Marie farther along the tableland. They wandered through small groves of low-growing junipers and paused occasionally on high points to survey the countryside.

They were a half mile from the rimrock when Bob stopped to study some small tracks in the sand. He finally realized he was looking at tortoise tracks, only a little different from the tracks of the eastern box turtle. The tortoise had disappeared into the cactus, where it was impossible to spot it.

As Bob rose to his feet, he called to Marie, who was standing on a rise a few yards to the front, "Let's go back."

Marie did not answer. He looked at her before calling louder. She had turned toward him, one finger resting against her lips to warn against making noise.

"What is it?" he whispered.

"Come here quick!" she answered softly.

7

As soon as Bob reached Marie's side, he
stopped in astonishment. A hundred yards away
six coyote puppies were wrestling among the
stalks of Indian paintbrush. They were perhaps
six weeks old, and although full of life and vigor,
they seemed unaware of a need to watch for
danger.

They looked like awkward foxes. Their sharp
noses and large ears were little different from

those of a fox. But their long legs and erratic lunges showed that their growing muscles had a long way to go before attaining the grace of a fox — or of an adult coyote.

The rollicking pups apparently were not aware of any such shortcomings, however. They piled into each other without hesitation, grabbing the first leg or tail that came into reach. None was allowed to lie unbothered more than a moment, for a pup sitting quietly by was a unanimous choice for attack.

Once Bob had seen two collie pups wrestling. These happy coyote pups appeared no different, except that there were three times as many.

"Where do you suppose the mother is?" Marie whispered.

"I don't know," Bob whispered back. "But I bet if we move, she'll come from somewhere."

He had no sooner finished saying this than a distant dog bark sounded. Suddenly a lone, high-pitched cry rose from a group of yucca plants a short distance uphill. The coyote pups stopped their play abruptly and scrambled into the tall grass. The ground seemed to swallow them. When the last had vanished, Marie spoke softly.

"I see their den hole."

"Where?" Bob asked automatically without attempting to conceal the fact that his sister had beaten him in this observation.

"Under that yucca clump with the flowers on it." Marie pointed cautiously. "Over there."

Bob saw it. Then he saw something else. A grown coyote limped into sight from the point where the warning cry had come. The coyote made no attempt at concealment, although Bob sensed that it had seen them. In fact, Bob noticed, the coyote detoured around the brush clumps in order to stay in the open as it limped up the slope.

Marie stood upright. "What do you suppose hurt that poor thing?"

Bob guessed that there was no longer any point in trying to stay concealed. "I bet nothing hurt her," he said.

"What do you mean?" Marie asked, glancing around at him.

"I've read about mother animals trying to lead danger away from their young ones."

"I don't believe it. Look at the way she's holding her front paw up. She's got it full of cactus or something."

"Do you think we can catch her now that she's crippled?" Bob asked.

"I sure do," Marie replied confidently. "Let's go."

With that, she broke into a sprint out of the junipers and up the slope. Bob ran after her. The coyote was no more than fifty steps away, and when it looked around at the two running children, the animal suddenly seemed to have even more difficulty limping along. Yet somehow it managed to stay twenty steps ahead of them.

"Let's wait a minute," Marie gasped. "Maybe it'll stop if we do."

It did. The coyote glanced back at them, and when they made no further move, it fell awkwardly to its side. That was too much for the sympathetic Marie.

"Oh, Bob," she cried, "it's hurt bad."

Bob could restrain himself no longer. He plunged forward. His sudden move seemed to surprise the coyote, for he was only five steps away when it bounded to its feet and leaped out of reach, this time with all four feet touching the ground. It bounded away with the sureness of a racing greyhound for a few more yards before slowing again to its limping walk. By now, however, the coyote was again fifty yards away.

Bob slowed to a stop. It was no use trying to beat this clever animal. Bob looked back to find Marie standing where she had stopped the first time.

"I'm convinced," she called cheerfully.

The coyote sat down on its haunches atop a boulder that overlooked the slope, while Bob and Marie walked back to where the coyote pups had disappeared.

"How can we get them out?" Marie asked as they picked their way through low clumps of hedgehog and prickly pear cactus. It was a miracle that they had not crashed into one on their wild chase.

"I don't know," Bob said. "Maybe we could dig them out."

Marie pointed to the rock outcroppings surrounding the den hole. "We could never dig through that rock."

Bob nodded in agreement. He was silent as they stood looking into the den hole.

"I bet Grandpa would know how to get them out," he said after a moment.

Marie brightened. "He sure would!" she said. "Let's go find him right now."

"All right," Bob said. "We'll have to hurry back, though, or the mother coyote might move them to a new den where we can't find them."

With spirits soaring at finding this unexpected treasure, the two hiked rapidly back toward the ranch. The farther they walked, however, the more serious Bob's thoughts became.

"You know," he remarked shortly, "I've been thinking that Grandma may not be too happy about our catching a coyote pup. After all, she's lost some chickens to coyotes."

"That's what I've been thinking, too," Marie said. "She might want Grandpa to get rid of them since they're so close to the ranch. It's probably this mama coyote that's been getting her chickens."

"You're right," Bob agreed.

They hiked along in silence for a time, letting themselves down the rocky slope by occasionally holding onto a pinyon limb for support. The morning was generally quiet, although once Bob heard distant barking again, and a magpie in the canyon below squawked at a squirrel busy in the scrubby trees. The crow-sized black and white bird was handsome, but it often made a nuisance of itself to other animal life by its loud harassment. The bird followed the squirrel for several minutes before tiring of its game, then flew off up canyon.

"You know," Bob said as they neared the canyon floor, "I think I know how we could get those pups out without hurting them."

"How?" Marie asked eagerly.

"We could smoke them out. We could burn some grass or leaves at the entrance to the den and let it fill up with smoke. Then we could hold a big feed sack over the hole, and the pups would run out into the sack."

"But they'd see the sack."

"Not if they had smoke in their eyes."

"What about the mother coyote?" Marie asked. "She might attack us."

"She might, but I don't think so if we've got a stick or something. She doesn't weigh over twenty pounds, I'll bet."

Marie had no more questions until they reached the barn. Then she thought of one.

"What will we do if Grandma Holmes won't let us keep them?"

"I've been thinking about that." Bob paused, then explained, "We could build a pen for them out in the woods somewhere and tame them. Maybe we could even teach them to do tricks. After Grandma saw they were no danger to the chickens, she wouldn't mind our keeping the pups."

Marie giggled. "I know what we could do."

"What?"

"We could teach them to eat peanut butter and jelly sandwiches instead."

Bob looked at her in exasperation. "Whoever heard of coyotes eating things like that?"

"There's always a first time," Marie said.

Bob still frowned. "You don't know about coyotes."

Undaunted, Marie retorted, "And coyotes don't know about peanut butter and jelly sandwiches."

As they neared the back porch, Bob told Marie, "We haven't got any time to argue. You get two empty feed sacks. I'll get the rest."

Grandma Holmes was busy with her canning as Bob walked into the kitchen. "What have you two kids been up to this morning?" she asked cheerily.

"Exploring," Bob answered.

"You missed all the excitement."

"What excitement?"

"The bounty hunter from the stock association came by. He thinks he has a coyote den spotted."

Although reluctant to ask the question, Bob finally did so. "Where'd the bounty hunter think the den was?"

"Not far," Grandma answered as she squeezed hot plum pulp through a strainer. "I think he said it was up there on the mesa just beyond where you and Marie were looking around."

Bob sucked in his breath, then whirled around. "I'll be back," he called over his shoulder. "I forgot something!"

"Don't you kids be late for lunch!" Grandma called after him.

Bob scarcely heard as he ran to Marie, who was folding a feed sack under her arm. Several were hanging on the fence.

"What's the matter with you?" she asked in surprise.

"Come on," he called. "We haven't a minute to lose!"

8

Bob wondered how long his knees would stand the pace as he led Marie back up the canyon slope. There was no talk. Neither felt like it after Bob had gasped, "Bounty hunter," to Marie. She knew from the look on his face what the hunter's probable target was.

They were both breathless before they were halfway to the top of the mesa. Bob soon stopped and leaned against a gnarled pine trunk to suck in fresh air. Marie paused a few feet below him, gasping for breath.

"Bob," she panted with a note of panic in her voice, "what — can we — do?"

"Get there — first!" Bob said.

Even as he spoke, he wondered what he could do when the hunter's dog pack found the den and began digging. Even if they didn't scratch their way inside before the hunter arrived, Bob knew he had little chance of talking the man out of killing the coyotes. After all, that was the way the hunter made his living — off coyote scalps.

"Slow down a little," Marie urged as Bob continued the climb.

"All right," he answered, knowing they would never be able to run all the way, anyway.

A few more minutes of steady climbing brought them to the rimrock. Bob stayed in the lead through the gully, and after another moment, they were back on the mesa.

The mesa allowed easier walking, and the two hiked rapidly through the rocky glades, which were bordered with thickets of brush. They were still several hundred yards away from the coyote den when they heard four shots in rapid succession, followed by excited dog barks. Holding up his hand for Marie to stop, Bob listened through the sound of his heavy breathing. Then two more shots came, and again the dogs barked wildly.

Dropping his hand, Bob nodded for Marie to continue. With a sick feeling deep inside him, he knew what he would find long before he reached the rise that overlooked the coyote den.

Marie dashed in front of him the last few steps to a place where she could see. "Oh, Bob," she sobbed, "he's killed them all!"

"Maybe just some of them," Bob said as he stopped by her side.

The two stood still in shock as they saw the bounty hunter straighten up over the carcass of one young coyote.

"He's just finished scalping them so he can collect the bounty payments," Bob said in a muffled whisper.

A little while before, it had seemed that the prospect of getting a live coyote pup for keeps was assured. Now that dream was suddenly shattered. The coyote family was dead.

"How do you guess he got them to come out where he could shoot them?" Marie asked, her voice breaking toward the last.

"He did what we were going to do. He built a fire and smoked them out — only he shot them when they ran out. We weren't even going to hurt them."

Anger began rising inside him to replace the shock. "We ought to go down there and beat those dogs down with sticks," he said hotly. But even while he was talking, he knew it was a foolish statement. The bounty hunter had every right to do what he was doing. It was lawful. To the people who hired him, his successful work meant more live lambs and calves with each dead coyote.

"Why don't we go stop them?" Marie asked.

Bob had never felt so helpless.

"There's no point to it," he muttered, snapping a twig off a nearby limb in frustration. "Anything we do would just get us in trouble — and Grandpa, too."

The hunter busied himself for a moment tossing the dead coyotes into thick brush so his milling dogs would not worry them and saturate their nostrils with the fresh coyote smell.

"Why's he doing that?" Marie asked.

"I think he wants his dogs to trail the coyote's mate so he can shoot him, too. The male coyote usually stays around and brings food to the den."

Quickly, the man got his dogs away from the den hole and urged them up the slope. Sure enough, another coyote dashed from the brush near the opposite crest.

"There he is!" Marie said excitedly, pointing to the male coyote disappearing over the ridge. "Do you suppose he'll get away?"

"He should," Bob said hopefully. "He's got a good start on the dogs. He ought to be able to run faster than they can through this rough country." Bob pointed toward the rocky hills in the distance. "He'll lose them out there."

They watched in silence as the man followed his dog pack out of sight.

Finally Marie spoke. "Let's go down and look. Maybe just one pup hid."

"There's not much chance of that," Bob said as they started forward. "The fire's still smoking. I bet it takes all day for the smoke to clear out of the den. If a pup stayed inside, it's probably suffocated."

The ground around the den was littered with hair tufts and scuffed by scratching dogs. The dead coyotes were out of sight in the brush. Bob was grateful for that. He didn't want to see the destruction this close.

"Look up there," Marie said, pointing to a wisp of smoke a dozen feet uphill. Her sudden arm movement apparently startled a magpie out of a pinyon thicket down the slope. The squawking bird flapped into the air.

Bob stepped up to the smoke streamer. "This is the air hole for the den," he said. "I read where coyotes burrow under a gopher hole or something and put their den right under it so they have ventilation."

"Coyotes are sure smart," Marie said sadly. "Who'd ever think they would know to do that?"

"It didn't help this family much. If any-thing, the air hole just drew smoke inside that much faster. It probably didn't take more than a minute or so before the coyotes had to scoot out for fresh air."

The magpie below them was still making its presence known. It dived into the brush and out again, squawking all the time.

"He sure does like to make noise," Marie said in irritation.

"I'd hate to be a squirrel with him around," Bob said as they took a final look at the den. "That hunter was sure careless. He didn't even bother to put out his fire."

Marie helped Bob scrape loose dirt over the fire embers. When no more smoke was left, they turned toward the ranch. After a few steps, how-ever, Marie stopped.

"You know what?" she said.

"What?"

"It's odd that a squirrel would be up here on the mesa so far away from the trees in the can-yon. They don't live in little bushes, do they?"

"Not as far as I know." Bob looked at the magpie now perched on a swaying twig.

After they had walked a few steps farther, Marie suddenly stopped again. "Say," she said excitedly, "you don't suppose that magpie . . ." She left the question unfinished.

Bob snapped his fingers. "It just might be," he said, as excited as she was. Both began trotting toward the bird. "We didn't see a squirrel down there. We just guessed it was one."

The bird shifted its attention to the running children. It allowed them to get within ten steps before leaping into the air and flapping away. Bob headed around one side of the bushes and Marie the other.

The next thing Bob knew, Marie screamed. As he turned toward her, he saw her racing down the slope as if a wild bull were on her heels.

9

There was no time to ask Marie what was chasing her. Snatching up a rock the size of a baseball, Bob raced around the bushes, half expecting to find a black bear or a bobcat after his sister. But there was nothing behind Marie!

Bob slowed, puzzled, until he spotted a small animal running a few steps ahead of her. Before he could gather any speed, Marie threw herself forward in a flying leap like a football player.

Her hands snatched up the fleeing little animal.

By the time Bob reached her, Marie was sitting with a coyote pup in her lap. One hand firmly gripped the little coyote's narrow nose to prevent a bite, and the other held its body close to hers so it could not escape.

"Wow!" Bob exclaimed as he slid to the ground in front of her. "So that's what it was."

The coyote pup took no pleasure from Marie's constricting arms. It struggled and twisted wildly, trying to free its nose of Marie's stubborn fingers. The struggles were useless, however, for Marie held on as if the young coyote were a part of her.

Finally the animal slowed its struggles to rest, and Marie began stroking its fur and talking quietly to calm it. The petting had the desired effect. As the pup relaxed, Marie opened her fingers slightly to let it breathe easier.

"Was this the only one?" Bob asked.

"I think so. At least, I didn't see any more." Marie slid her fingertips through the pup's soft fur to comb it. "How do you suppose the dogs missed this one?"

"I don't know. Maybe the mother coyote was moving her pups to a new place after she found us at her den. But the dogs ran up before they got very far, and all except this one scooted back to the den."

Marie was still too elated over her good fortune to care very much just how it had happened, however. She only half listened to Bob's theory.

"Isn't he beautiful?" she said, smiling, as she studied the frightened pup's face. "He looks about like a police dog pup. He's even the same color."

The little coyote settled into her lap, more from exhaustion than friendliness, and continued its heavy panting.

"How old do you suppose he is?" Marie asked.

"He couldn't be much more than a few weeks, or you couldn't have run fast enough to catch him." Bob could hold back his big question no longer. "What'll you take for him?"

Marie snapped her head up, still smiling. "Are you crazy? I wouldn't take anything for him. He's mine."

Bob helped her pet the bewildered pup. Apparently it was unsure about what might result from all this attention by humans. Each quick hand movement scared it, and it tried several times to rear out of Marie's hands.

"What're we going to name him?" Bob asked.

"I don't know," Marie answered happily, her thoughts still busy with the little tangle of furry legs and ears in her lap. Suddenly she looked up, her brows pushed together in a frown. "What do you mean *we?*" she asked indignantly. "What am *I* going to name him, you mean. I caught him all by myself."

Bob couldn't argue with that statement. He dropped the matter until he could think of some new way to claim part-ownership.

After a few minutes, when the pup had calmed again, Bob said, "We'd better get back home. Grandma Holmes told us to be back by lunchtime."

Marie followed as Bob picked his way through the center of the thicket that had hidden the pup. This was the hardest possible route home, but Bob wanted to make sure that no more pups were hidden there. By the time he got to the opposite side, he was satisfied that there were no more.

Picking up the feed sacks, which Marie had dropped, Bob now took an easier path toward the ranch, walking along open ground.

"What do you suppose Grandma Holmes is going to say?" he asked.

"About what?"

"About our bringing a coyote home for a pet."

Marie was silent for a time. Finally she said, "You don't suppose she'd take him away from us, do you?"

Bob noticed with satisfaction that she had slipped and used "us" instead of "me." He looked at the awkward little pup in her arms.

"Well, he probably doesn't weigh five pounds now, but she'll be thinking about the time he grows up and is big enough to kill chickens."

"Oh, she just can't make us give him up!" Marie said fiercely, as if saying this firmly enough would make it more true. Marie was apprehensive now, and her steps slowed instinctively, as if she could protect the pup longer by taking more time to get to the ranch. "We've got to do something," she pleaded. "We just can't let anything happen to him."

A plan had begun to form in Bob's mind. It might just work. Marie seemed to read his thoughts, and her face brightened when he spoke.

"I think I've got it, Marie."

"What?"

"We won't take the pup back to the ranch."

"But we've got to take care of him and make him tame."

"We can, but we don't have to do it at the ranch." Bob pointed to the rimrock already within sight. "You know that rock cliff at the edge of the mesa?"

Marie nodded.

"Well, we could stack up loose rocks and make a pen against the bottom of the cliff so the pup couldn't get out. We could water him and feed him and pet him until he was nice and tame."

"Then Grandma Holmes wouldn't get rid of him because we could show her he was tame and wouldn't bother the chickens." Marie's voice sounded hopeful once more.

"Well, it's worth a try."

Bob said no more as he led Marie down the gully through the rimrock. When they reached the talus slope, he selected a route along the cliff, and they followed it for a few yards.

"This ought to do," he said after a moment. "These scrubby pines will hide the pen and keep it shaded, and there's plenty of sandstone slabs around."

As Marie held the pup and kept an eye on the ranch house, which could be seen plainly from this point, Bob began stacking stones. He made a circular pen no larger than a baby's playpen.

"There's one condition," he announced after a moment, "since you're not helping."

"I can't help," Marie said. "I've got to hold him." She looked at Bob suspiciously. "What's the condition?"

"From now on, it's half and half. Half the pup is mine."

It was a hard bargain for Marie. She looked unhappy about it, but she couldn't excite the pup by putting it into the feed sack now that it was calm. The pen had to be built, and she recognized the need for Bob's help in taking care of the pup.

"Oh-h-h," she sighed in resignation, "all right. He's half yours."

Bob smiled at his victory, then got back to work. He sloped the pen sides inward as he built them up so the pup could not scramble out. He had seen pups run up rock walls. He made the wall nearly three feet high, planning to close off the top with a single sandstone slab, an effective lid to prevent the pup's escape.

"Can you see Grandma Holmes down there yet?" he asked. "We're sure late for lunch."

"She's on the back porch," Marie said. "She's staring right up here."

Bob looked up from his work. "She can't see us, can she?"

"No, the trees are too thick."

The pen was finished now. Bob hastily checked to make certain there were no cracks between the rocks that would allow the pup to squeeze through. Satisfied with his inspection, he folded the feed sacks into a comfortable bed and climbed from the pen.

Marie let the little coyote slide free of her arms onto the rock floor. She and Bob watched as the pup sank to its stomach and pushed itself against the stacked rocks. Its disheveled fur, moist from Marie's perspiring arms, seemed to indicate its low spirits. It was bewildered and scared. Its thirsty tongue hung out, and it panted heavily.

"We've got to bring a pan of water up here as soon as we can," Marie said.

"If Grandma Holmes'll let us," Bob said as he laid the last stone over the top of the pen. "She may not let us out of the house the rest of the day since we're so late."

As they hurried down the slope, sliding on loose shale and pushing through stiff clumps of greasewood, Marie asked, "How long do you suppose the pup can live without water?"

"I don't know," answered Bob. "Probably not for very long."

10

As Bob and Marie stepped onto the back porch, they heard Grandma Holmes talking through the screen door.

"I was about to send for the sheriff to search for you two," she said with mock seriousness. "What've you been up to?"

Bob and Marie pretended great interest in the wash pan on the porch. As he sloshed cooling water onto his face and washed his hands for lunch, Bob answered Grandma's question.

"We went up on the mesa and found where that bounty hunter had killed a whole family of coyotes."

"Did he kill all the pups?" Grandma Holmes asked. She stepped out to join them and make sure no face or hand areas remained unwashed.

Marie started to say something, but Bob beat her to it. "We got up there where we could see just as he finished scalping them. We watched him throw the mother coyote and her pups into the brush."

"How many pups did she have?"

"We couldn't tell from where we were," Bob said quite truthfully.

Grandma Holmes took the washrag from Marie and began a thorough cleaning of her dusty face. Perspiration had made streaks down it.

"My," Grandma Holmes remarked, "you two must have really had a hike judging from the way you're messed up."

She finished Marie's face and began work on her arms. "How'd you get all the hair on your arms? It looks as if you've been crawling through a coyote den."

Bob brought his head up in surprise to look at Marie's arms. Scattered hairs were stuck to her skin. Bob quickly tried to explain.

"We've been climbing through a lot of bushes

up on the slope. It could be bits of their bark."

"It could be, all right," Grandma said. Bob studied her face to see if the smile that seemed to be at the corners of her mouth was really there. "But it's not."

Fortunately, Grandma had no more to say about the subject as she led them inside.

"Grandpa still gone?" Marie asked as they slid into chairs at the kitchen table.

"Yes," Grandma answered. "He ought to be back most any time now, though."

Bob hardly noticed what was on the table; all his thoughts were about the coyote pup and its condition. It seemed that Marie was thinking about the same thing. Even the big dish of apple cobbler, cooled with icy milk, was not the treat it should have been.

As they finished eating, Grandma said, "My, you two sure have been in a hurry. Either my food's powerful good, or you're in a hurry to get somewhere."

Neither Bob nor Marie had anything to say. Bob was afraid he might say the wrong thing, so he didn't take a chance. He just nodded absently.

"You know what would be nice for you to do this afternoon?" Grandma Holmes asked as she began clearing the table.

Bob was alarmed. Anything that would prevent their watering the coyote pup — even for a little while — might be disastrous. Thoroughly concerned, Bob had a quick vision of the pup stretched out lifeless.

"Could we do it late this afternoon?" Marie asked quickly.

"Well," Grandma Holmes said, "if necessary. I wouldn't want you to put it off too late, though. Later when it gets cool, the snakes come out of the rock cracks."

"What do you want us to do?" Bob asked as he sidled toward the door. Marie had already backed to the screen.

"You remember those Oregon grapes your Grandpa showed you last night out by the fence? There's a big patch of them up on the slope across the creek. I think it would be nice if you two gathered a bucketful for jelly."

Grandma Holmes was not prepared for the joyful reception of this news. She looked up in amazement as both children gave a "Yippee!" and scrambled out the door. Some empty tin pails were sitting on the porch. Bob and Marie each snatched up one, then headed toward the barn.

"I know where some tin cans are," Marie said in a low tone as they crossed the backyard. "One of them will make a good watering pan."

"I don't know what we're going to feed him," Bob said. "I guess he's been weaned by his mother because he's so big."

"What do coyotes eat when they're wild?"

"Mostly rats and rabbits, according to all I've read."

"How're we going to catch rabbits?"

"We can't." Bob thought a moment more. "Come to think of it, though, Grandpa mentioned that the coyotes get in his watermelons and cantaloupes every summer. We could take a little watermelon up there."

Marie snapped her fingers. "You know what else?" she said suddenly. "We've got all the rats the pup can use." She pointed to the barn. "The rattraps Grandpa sets out by the feed sacks — I bet he takes a half dozen rats out of them some days."

During the next five minutes, they found two dead rats in the traps. They reset the traps and got a clean tin can, then headed for the creek below the coyote's pen. After they had filled one pail with water and started up the slope, Bob had another thought.

"Grandpa's going to get suspicious when he starts finding his rattraps empty."

"Well," said Marie hopefully, "maybe he'll just think he's trapped all the rats that live in the barn."

"Could be," Bob said. "But from what he told us yesterday, there are more rats and chipmunks around here now than there've been for years. I think he'll begin to suspect something's going on."

"There's one way to be safe."

"What's that?"

"Well, if we tame the pup fast enough, and walk home someday with him tagging along like a real dog, Grandpa'll have to let us keep him — just as if he was a real dog." Marie grabbed a limb and pulled herself up the steep slope. "He's just got to," she insisted.

After the hard climb, Bob was relieved to find the pen just as they had left it. The trees did a good job of shading it, and only a few spots of sunlight touched the stacked rock. Lifting off the covering rock, Bob looked inside. Marie peered over his shoulder.

The coyote pup looked up with no great show of interest. It was too thirsty to move from the cool rock on which it lay. Bob quickly filled the tin can with water from the pail and set the can in front of the pup's nose.

With a happy little bark that sounded like "Kip," the pup popped erect and began drinking. It was so thirsty that it paid no attention to the hands stroking its fur. Marie soon began scratching its head gently with an index finger, and when the pup had drunk its fill of water, it lifted its head high to take advantage of the pleasing sensation.

"Why don't we call him Kip?" Marie asked. "That's the only thing he can say."

Bob thought a moment. "Kip, the coyote," he said. "I guess that's as good a name as any."

After another moment of scratching, however, the pup recovered its natural fear of humans. It crouched and crawled quickly to the opposite side of the pen. When Bob reached over to pet it, the young coyote drew back its upper lip in a snarl that uncovered needlelike teeth.

"Take it easy, Kip," Bob said in a soothing voice. "I'm not going to hurt you."

"We better leave him alone for a while," Marie suggested.

Bob nodded. "I guess that is better than getting a finger chewed off."

Marie picked up the two dead rats from the pail she carried. Holding them gingerly by their tails, she dropped them in front of the pup. It only glanced at them before looking back at the two faces staring over the rock wall.

"How're we ever going to tame him if we leave him up here in this pile of rocks all by himself?" Marie asked. She reached cautiously toward the pup, but it snarled again.

Both she and Bob were deep in thought as they moved down the slope, picking the juicy berries of Oregon grape, a low-growing shrub with spiny leaves resembling those of holly trees.

On the third visit to Kip, Bob and Marie found a happy surprise. The coyote pup rose to his feet when they looked into his pen. Bob thought he also detected a wagging tail, but he couldn't be sure. However, when Marie reached down to pat Kip's head, the pup backed out of reach.

"Let's not hurry him," Bob whispered as he refilled the water can and placed it in the pen.

Kip had not touched the rats while Bob and Marie were present on the first two visits. After they left, however, he had eaten them. Now Marie laid another rat from one of the barn traps near Kip. To the children's satisfaction, Kip waited only a moment before pouncing on the rat and beginning his meal. They made no attempt to disturb him until he had finished.

When he settled to his stomach and began licking his nose and lips, Marie extended her hand toward him again. She took care to keep her hand in front of him to prevent alarming him. It seemed for a moment that Kip was getting ready to snap at her. His lips drew back in a slight snarl, but suddenly this show of belligerence melted away. The pup stuck out his shiny black nose to meet Marie's fingertips.

Kip allowed Marie to scratch the hair above his nose. Then she began smoothing the hair on his head. Before long, she whispered, "He's relaxing now as if he likes it." After another moment, she stroked the fur along his back. The pup seemed to like the gentle petting and soft words of encouragement.

Marie kept this up for a quarter of an hour, until Bob remarked, "We'd better get back down to the house before Grandma Holmes gets to wondering where we've gone."

Marie gave Kip a final pat and withdrew her

hand. The pup rose to his feet and stood watching them until they put the sandstone lid on his pen.

During the climb down the slope, Marie told Bob about something that had been worrying her. "You know those holes near the top of the pen," she said, "the ones where the lid doesn't fit too good?" Bob nodded. "Well, what's to keep something from crawling through and getting Kip while we're gone?"

"Like what?"

"A horned owl maybe, or even a rattlesnake. They could crawl in there and bite him."

"I don't know what's to stop them," Bob said. "It's just a chance we'll have to take."

"How long do you think it'll take to make him really tame?" Marie asked as she stopped before a low pinyon limb. She pushed the limb aside, then spread her hand. It was sticky with pine resin.

"I don't know," answered Bob. "It might take just a few days. But it might take two or three weeks to really tame him. He's still a wild animal mostly."

The next visit to Kip was less rewarding. The pup seemed to revert to his wild instincts again. He allowed petting only after five minutes of soothing words from the two children.

The fifth visit, however, was all that Bob and

Marie could wish for. They were later than usual, for they had made a fruitless search of the barn's rattraps. Finally they had given up trying to find a rat, and had taken a few table scraps and a cantaloupe from the field behind the barn.

This time Kip was on his hind legs with his front feet stretched up toward them when they looked into the pen. Bob broke open the cantaloupe while Kip ate the table scraps, and then Bob handed him pieces of the juicy melon. He liked them and didn't stop eating until the cantaloupe was half gone.

Kip offered no resistance now to petting, and when he rolled to his back and Marie tickled his stomach, the young coyote appeared to love it. He rolled and playfully nipped at her fingers.

"Let's take him out," Marie said. "He won't run away."

Bob was dubious for a moment, but Kip's playful actions convinced him it was all right. Marie lifted the pup out and set him on the ground between them. In another moment, Kip showed that he was first a pup and then a coyote. He wrestled their shoes, hands, and sleeves with all the abandon of a delighted collie pup, slowing his play only after he grew tired.

"Let's take him home today," Marie suggested.

Bob studied Kip for a moment. "It sure

would be nice," he agreed. "But what if he starts acting up the way he did yesterday? Grandma Holmes will be sure he's nothing but a wild animal; she'll be afraid he might hurt us or at least catch her chickens."

Marie agreed reluctantly. They put Kip back in his pen.

During the next three days, Bob and Marie managed to visit Kip each morning and afternoon. Several times their grandparents gave them errands and small jobs that threatened to prevent a visit, but each time they managed to complete the tasks in time to allow regular feeding.

One afternoon Grandma Holmes met them near the barn as they returned from visiting Kip. She looked at them closely and then smiled.

"My, you two are the exploringest children I've ever seen," she said. "If I didn't know better, I'd think you had some playmates or something across the creek."

Startled by her uncomfortably close guess, Bob remained silent, and when Marie started to say something, he gave her a warning glance. She saw what he meant and said nothing as they followed their grandmother to the house.

Grandpa was not home at dusk when they sat down to eat. "He went out to check some fences across the creek," Grandma Holmes explained as she drew up her chair.

The meal was nearly over before they heard Grandpa's steps on the back porch. When he entered the kitchen, he had a peculiar look on his face. It seemed as if he had just learned some special secret.

"Why're you so late tonight?" Grandma Holmes asked.

"I was getting ready to come to the house when I noticed some buzzards circling up near the rimrock."

Marie gasped. Bob stopped his fork halfway to his mouth.

"Which rimrock?" he asked.

Grandpa nodded toward the slope where Kip's pen was located. "I walked up there to see if a yearling might've got itself into trouble."

"Did you find one?" Bob asked quickly.

"No, but I did find something."

"What?" Marie interrupted.

"Oh, just an old dead jackrabbit."

Somehow Grandpa seemed to be too nonchalant, Bob thought as he continued eating. Before long, however, Grandpa had a question.

"What've you two been up to this afternoon?" he asked as he spread butter onto hot corn bread.

"Just playing," Marie said. Bob nodded.

"It's too bad you two don't have somebody to play with out here. Or at least a pet."

Bob and Marie kept their eyes on him as he continued talking.

"It sure would be nice if you had a pup for a pet." He finished his piece of corn bread and started on another. "It'd be even nicer if you had a wild pet."

Marie was having a hard time containing herself. "Like what, Grandpa?"

"Oh, I don't know. Some kind of wild, fuzzy little old animal." He looked up from his corn bread. "Like a turtle or a snake, maybe."

"They're not fuzzy," Marie said.

"Well then, maybe something like a little old lonesome coyote puppy." Grandpa's eyes twinkled as he spoke.

"That would be nice," Bob said with fast-rising apprehension. "But where'd we get one?"

"Why, I suppose the best place would be from wherever you happened to run across a coyote puppy." Grandpa's eyes showed a definite smile now.

"Where would that be?"

"Well, one place might be a pile of rocks up on the rim. I just happened to find a coyote puppy up there awhile ago. He looked so lonesome for somebody to talk to that I figured I'd better bring him on down here for company."

Bob jumped to his feet. "Grandpa, you've got Kip!"

Grandpa's face was a broad grin now. "Well, the pup didn't say his name was Kip, but I wouldn't be surprised if he knew some folks right close by."

"Can we keep him?" Bob and Marie asked at practically the same time as if they had rehearsed it for a school play.

Grandpa glanced at Grandma Holmes. Her face began to lose its look of surprise.

"Well," she said, and then paused as if deep in thought. "I'm trying to think of some reason why you shouldn't." Bob and Marie were in agony before she finally got it said. "I guess I can't think of any reason why he shouldn't be one of the family. Can you think of a reason, Grandpa?"

Grandpa shook his head, then said softly, "He's in the woodbox on the porch."

12

The next morning Grandpa constructed a permanent box and wire-enclosed run on the back porch for Kip. While Bob helped his grandfather, Marie cuddled Kip and played with him.

By the time the pen was ready, Kip seemed thoroughly at home in the ranch yard. There were no threats to the young coyote here, and he seemed to know it instinctively. He even allowed Grandpa to pat his head during the morning.

"Let's see how much he weighs," Grandpa said when he had finished working on the run.

Marie lifted Kip into the pan hanging from the small vegetable scales on the porch. Grandpa looked at the scales with mock disapproval.

"Little pup," he said, "you wouldn't even weigh as much as a good cantaloupe if you were soaking wet."

Bob looked at the needle on the scales. It barely reached the three-pound mark.

Weight made no difference, however, thought Bob, as he lifted Kip off the scales. Handsomeness made up for the lack of pounds. Kip's long fur was generally the light gray color of soft ashes left from a campfire, although his throat and underparts were nearly white. The black hairs at his tail's end formed a distinctive tip.

The next few days seemed to be as satisfying to Kip as they were to Bob and Marie. Much playing and petting delighted the pup, and he grew more attached to his keepers by the hour.

"You'd think that pup never had a coyote for a mother, the way he tags along with you two," said Grandma Holmes one evening when Kip struggled up into Marie's lap.

The family was sitting around the fireplace. The high altitude of northern Arizona made a fire a comfort on many summer evenings.

"Why don't we move Kip's sleeping box into

our bedroom, Grandma?" Marie asked. "He's nice and clean and wouldn't get anything dirty."

"I'll think about it," Grandma said without committing herself.

Grandpa, reaching over to scratch Kip's chin, remarked, "That might be a mean trick to play on Kip."

Marie looked shocked. "What do you mean, Grandpa? We could watch over him here in the house, and nothing could hurt him."

"Well, I'll tell you, Marie. It's like this. Suppose there was a little girl who had lived all her life in a big city apartment house, and never had a chance to get used to life in the woods and to cold weather. Suppose you set this girl down in the middle of a wilderness all of a sudden. Her body just wouldn't be prepared for it. She'd likely catch a cold right away, then get something serious like pneumonia."

"But coyotes are different," Marie protested.

"Not when it comes to something like that," her grandfather said. "There must be thousands of cats and dogs that die each year because their owners bring them in out of the cold. Their bodies and fur have no chance to build up resistance against the cold and the wind. Then some night when the owners leave such a cat or dog outside too long, it gets sick and dies, and the owners can't understand why."

He paused and then continued, "If you want to keep Kip healthy, you've got to let him live outdoors as much as possible."

This was unpleasant but true, and Bob realized it. He could see disappointment in Marie's face, but she, too, recognized the common sense of it.

Over the next few days, Bob found that Grandpa's advice was very good. Kip stayed healthy and seemed to grow a measurable amount each day. His fur became coarser like an adult's, and his legs grew long and lanky, capable of a coyote's characteristic speed.

He ate an amazing variety of food. Almost any small thing that moved was suitable prey, and anything that was palatable to humans was as popular on Kip's menu. The young coyote sampled citrus fruits, berries, watermelons, grasshoppers, horned lizards, minnows, eggs, mesquite beans, plums, and the fruit of the prickly pear cactus.

Like all young creatures, human or animal, Kip loved to romp and play. Curious and eager, he liked exploring under rocks, behind bushes, or in holes as much as Bob and Marie liked exploring around the ranch. He liked playing with Bob and Marie, too. They were always cooperative playmates, though some of his other acquaintances were not.

One such acquaintance was the testy old

Plymouth Rock rooster ruling the barnyard chickens. Kip tried several times to get the cock to join his play. He scampered past it or stalked up with hips held aside, inviting a game of tag, but the aloof cock would have none of it.

Once, when Kip extended his nose as a sign of friendship, the old cock pecked him viciously. The startled pup scrambled out of range. He nursed a sore nose over the next several hours, and kept a wary eye out for his barnyard enemy.

One morning Bob saw the big rooster ruffle its neck like a belligerent gamecock when Kip trotted across the yard. The young coyote allowed the rooster to come no closer than four or five steps before scampering away from its threatening beak.

"Look at that, Grandpa!" Bob said. "That old bully should pick on something his own size." Bob reached to the ground, seized a corncob, and flung it at the rooster.

"Be careful now," Grandpa said. "That's the only rooster we've got just now, and I don't want him killed." Grandpa pointed to the light-footed Kip. "That pup can always stay out of reach. In fact, if I know coyotes, I think we'll see a surprised rooster one of these days."

During the next few days, the rooster grew more arrogant. Each time Kip came near the feeding hens, the old cock would give chase, bobbing along with drooping wings and ruffled neck until Kip scampered beyond reach. With each chase, the rooster grew more confident of its ability to bluff and threaten, for Kip's retreat was longer each time. Bob noticed, however, that Kip allowed his tormentor to stay close behind a little longer during each chase.

One morning the rooster headed for Kip the minute Grandpa and the two children stepped off the back porch with table scraps and chicken feed in hand. Kip had joined the three, trotting along at Marie's heels. He had done nothing to raise the ire of the crusty old cock other than just appear.

Kip stopped short a few feet from the porch and stared at the oncoming rooster with detachment, as if he really didn't see it. The rooster's anger mounted with each step, and when it seemed certain that it was too late to dodge away, Kip managed to do so.

With studied casualness, Kip trotted aside, toward the cluster of hens eager for their morning feed. The hens scattered before him. Then, as if to annoy the rooster further, Kip snatched a mouthful of feathers from the nearest hen.

This action had the desired effect. The furious rooster bore down on Kip at full speed. Kip headed out of the barnyard and across the open flat by the creek.

"Grandpa," Marie cried, "stop him before he hurts Kip."

Grandpa put his hand on Marie's shoulder. "Wait a minute. The rooster won't bother Kip. Watch."

Bob could not tolerate the bullying any longer. He snatched up several rocks and started to join the pursuit, but he was stopped by a new tactic of Kip's.

The fleeing Kip let the rooster come within inches of him. The rooster drew back its neck to aim a furious peck at Kip's tail. Then it happened.

Kip reversed himself in a twinkle. Before the rooster realized that Kip was now the pursuer, the pup was on top of it. The next two seconds were a blur of action, filled with dust and flying feathers. Kip gave the rooster no chance to launch an attack of its own. He pressed the cock so hard that it had no way of stopping the loss of its splendid tail feathers except by fleeing.

The cock's humiliation was complete in front of the hens. They watched in surprise as their once proud hero fled squawking through them in an effort to escape.

Kip did not pause, however. The chase continued around the barnyard and back again. Finally, the frantic rooster flapped heavily to the toolshed roof. It just barely managed to gain the top with the aid of its churning feet and beak, which dug into the wooden shingles.

As the bedraggled cock settled to its feet, Bob saw that it had only two or three tail feathers left. It would be weeks before the rooster regained its lost feathers — and its dignity.

Grandpa chuckled as the triumphant Kip trotted back toward them. "I thought it was coming. It's happened too many times before. I've heard of more than one dog getting the same trick played on him by a sly old coyote, who led him on and on and then turned on him all of a sudden."

As Kip pranced around them, Grandpa added, "There was a dog that kept worrying a little coyote at a ranch where I worked once. The dog kept getting closer and braver each time the coyote showed up near the barn. Then one night there was the worst commotion you ever heard behind the barn. When I looked out of the bunkhouse, that dog was racing across the yard with six coyotes after him, and he didn't stop till he got under the porch where they couldn't get to him. That little coyote had gone out and brought in some buddies, then ambushed that dog."

Bob knew it was ridiculous to think coyotes could understand human talk. But he would have bet his pocketknife that Kip had a sly smile on his face as Grandpa told the story.

The few weeks of midsummer, when Kip's growth picked up momentum, were trying ones for Bob and Marie; for Kip, they were even more trying. It was a period when Kip's adolescent muscles and bones had not yet gained the firmness and responsiveness of adulthood. As a result, his awkwardness, and his incessant curiosity, caused never-ending troubles.

His main troubles were not necessarily caused

by his life on the ranch, although he gained little favor with Grandma Holmes by slipping into Marie's bed whenever he got a chance. Kip's real troubles were common to all wild coyotes.

For a while, it seemed that Kip got into every possible predicament, a new one each day. One morning he nosed the top off one of Grandpa's beehives down by the creek. He had just dipped his nose into the combs of honey, made from spring cliff rose blossoms, when he also managed to push the hive off its stand.

Bob and Marie were wading in the shallow creek at the time. They saw the swarming bees erupt like smoke from a volcano only yards away. Yelping, Kip raced toward Bob for protection, bringing a few thousand furious bees with him.

"Duck under the water!" Bob screamed to Marie.

The two dove underneath the surface. But that tactic was good for only a few seconds; their lungs soon strained for fresh air. Climbing to his feet again, Bob began splashing water over Marie. She splashed back, and Kip wasted no time getting into the protecting spray.

After a full five minutes of the wild splashing, the bees seemed to be discouraged. Bob herded Marie downstream cautiously so as not to attract any more bees. Hundreds of them floated on the water surface like so many cottonwood seeds. Most would drift to the bank and crawl out to dry.

Kip showed none of his usual exuberance now. He waded quietly between Marie and Bob, his tail floating on the surface, his face showing his chagrin.

Early the next morning, Kip found a new reason for chagrin. Bob was awakened at dawn again by a pack rat on the bedroom floor. This time the rat had found a new attraction.

Bob's scalp tingled in fright when his sleep-fogged eyes first saw it — a snake sliding stealthily across the floor. Sleep left him instantly. His eyes cleared, and then he made out the long thin shape of his black leather belt. The pack rat, holding one end in its mouth, was triumphantly dragging it toward the closet floor exit. Bob had been awakened by the sound of the shiny metal buckle hitting the floor.

Bob popped out of bed. The surprised rat held onto its prize, reluctant to part with such a hard-earned treasure. But Bob, snatching up a shoe and flinging it at the rat, soon convinced the little animal that retreat was wise.

"Let's get Kip after it!" Marie exclaimed, having awakened in time to see the fleeing rodent.

"Hey, what goes on here?" Grandma Holmes called as the two pajama-clad youngsters sprinted through the kitchen to the back porch.

Kip was waiting at the screen door. He had already been up for hours. Bob snatched him up and ducked around the house toward the route the pack rat had to take to its nest. He was in time. The rat had not paused under the house, but was scurrying across the open yard.

Bob dropped Kip three feet behind the pack rat. The two animals raced across the yard toward the cactus clumps where the rat lived. The speedy young coyote nearly caught the rat inches from its nest. But the little animal fled under the cactus and disappeared into the tunnel of debris that it had constructed.

Kip was traveling too fast for dodging. He plowed into the cactus-studded tunnel. With a series of pained yelps, he veered aside and came to a halt. Burying his face between his front feet, he churned frantically, trying to pull out the scores of hard spines. It did no good.

Grandma Holmes relieved Kip's pain over the next half hour as she sat on the back porch with Kip upturned between her knees and tweezers in her hand. So absorbed did she become in her work that the breakfast biscuits burned black.

The pack rat episode should end Kip's predicaments, Bob suggested to his grandfather later that morning as he helped replace stable boards in the barn. The old boards had absorbed cattle sweat, and the salt left in the wood had attracted a porcupine. The animal had gnawed the thick boards, once strong enough to hold a bull, into scallop-edged slats that could be easily broken.

"There aren't many animals as pesky as a porcupine," Grandpa remarked as he sawed. Bob held the board's short end. "People think a porcupine's harmless because he moves so slow, but offhand I guess he kills more trees than all other wild animals put together."

"How's he do that?" Bob asked.

"His main food is the inner bark of trees. One porcupine may take up in a big yellow pine and gnaw his way up and down and around it until all the inner bark's gone. Then the tree starves to death because all its food and water are supposed to pass through that inner bark."

"Well, there's a lot of trees," Bob said.

"There's a lot of porcupines, too. I know a fellow over in Oak Creek Canyon who trapped fourteen porcupines out of an apple orchard in one year. They would've killed his little orchard in no time if he hadn't seen them. Then worse," Grandpa said ruefully as he paused to wipe sweat off his forehead, "they cause a man like me to do all this repair work when I shouldn't have to."

"How're you going to stop this porcupine?"

"I've tried to trap him several times, but so far I haven't had much luck. If I could ever catch him in here at work, I'd get him, but he drifts in every once in a while and drifts out again before I know he's been here."

The more Bob thought about the vandal porcupine, the more interested he became in devising some way to surprise it. Kip would certainly be able to smell out the lumbering animal anytime it was near or in hiding.

As a consequence, Bob and Marie took Kip on barn explorations several times each day for the next several days. Bob pushed Kip's nose against the boards marked by porcupine teeth to acquaint the pup with the animal's scent. However, Kip had little interest in the boards.

Bob had given up hope of surprising the porcupine when one morning, as he and his sister headed toward the creek, Marie pointed to the dusty ground. "Look at these funny tracks, Bob."

The tracks led to the barn. Whatever had made them had come from a pinyon pine grove during the night. Bob searched the dust near the tracks to see if there were any return tracks. There were none.

"It must still be in the barn," Bob said with growing excitement. "Let's look."

One look was enough. A fat porcupine sat before a stable board casually gnawing it to dust. It ignored the two children and the coyote pup.

"Let's get Grandpa!" Bob exclaimed, heading toward the ranch house.

They were halfway back to the barn with Grandpa trotting behind when Bob realized that Kip had never left the barn. With a burst of speed, Bob sprinted through the barn door in time to see the inevitable.

Kip was pushing out an exploratory nose toward the porcupine. The animal looked at Kip, giving no indication of displeasure. It swung one side toward the pup. Then its quill-studded tail slapped forward with surprising speed, catching Kip full in the nose. Kip recoiled as if driven by a powerful spring. His nose looked like a pincushion stuck with several dozen white quills resembling big round toothpicks.

Wild with pain, Kip raced from the barn and across the yard. Once he started to slide his nose along the dust in an effort to relieve his hurts, but this drove the barbs deeper, and the frantic pup began running in erratic circles.

Grandpa permanently ended the porcupine's destructiveness by picking up a board and hitting the animal's weak spot, its supersensitive nose.

"Catch Kip," he instructed Bob. "Quickly!"

This was no easy matter. Kip seemed afraid that handling might make the quills hurt more. Bob and Marie managed to converge on the circling pup, however, and Bob carried Kip, struggling wildly, to the porch. Grandpa met them with pliers in hand.

Fortunately for Kip, he had been recoiling when the porcupine's tail hit him, and none of the quills was deeper than a quarter inch. While Bob and Marie held the writhing pup firmly, Grandpa jerked out the quills.

"There aren't many meaner things that can happen to a wild animal than to get a snout full of porcupine quills," Grandpa said as he worked. "Instead of working out of the skin like a thorn or a cactus spine, a quill will work deeper. It sounds impossible, but a quill will work all the way through a leg or a nose and come out the other side."

"Really?" Marie said.

"Yes, really. When I was a kid, I got slapped on the arm by a porcupine. I thought I'd pulled out all the quills, but I'd missed two little bitty ones. Two or three weeks later, they'd worked all the way through my arm and poked out the other side. I pulled them out then."

Kip's suffering diminished as the row of quills on the steps grew longer. His struggles stopped, but his tight face muscles and quick winces as each quill was yanked free showed that the procedure was far from painless.

"Each of these quills is covered by little barbs you can hardly see," Grandpa explained. "The barbs point away from the tip of the quill, and every time the muscles move and make the tip dig in a little deeper, the barbs anchor the quill in place so it can't back out. A grizzly bear with a face full of quills is just as helpless as a coyote pup."

Bob picked up one of the quills with his free hand and scraped his thumbnail down its side. It felt like rough sandpaper.

"Say," Marie said, "I read once about a porcupine throwing its quills like darts. How can it do that?"

"Well," Grandpa said, "it really can't throw them like that. It just seems that way because the quills fly off so easy. They hardly have to touch you to stick. Then, too, when a porcupine gets to thrashing its tail around, the loose quills are slung free, and they'll stick into anything close."

"How many quills do you suppose a porcupine has?" Marie asked.

"Too many — twenty or thirty thousand."

After removing the last quill, Grandpa used a wad of cotton to dab antiseptic on Kip's wounds. Kip cringed at this treatment, too, but he seemed to know that Grandpa was trying to help, and his struggling was slight.

During the rest of the day, Kip stuck close to the heels of Bob and Marie. For the moment, it seemed that his curiosity was fully satisfied. Bob guessed, however, that the troubles of the playful young coyote were not over.

14

Bob and Marie had owned Kip for six weeks when the bounty hunter drove into the ranch yard one morning. He was the same man they had seen in Sedona at the bus station, the one who had destroyed the coyote family.

Bob could hear the man's greyhounds yelping in the back of the truck when it stopped. The sign that read "Robin Parker, Predator Control" was hard to see through the dust coating.

"Where's Kip?" Bob asked Marie as soon as he recognized the man's truck.

"I don't know. I haven't seen him for a while."

Grandpa was already on his way to talk to the man. Bob was worried.

"Go find Kip," he told Marie. "I'll go out there and make sure that man doesn't let his dogs out."

"Now, hold on," Grandma Holmes cautioned. "Your grandfather won't let the hunter turn his dogs out around the ranch house, and I'm sure the man wouldn't be that rude anyway."

"Rude!" Bob exclaimed. "He murdered Kip's whole family, didn't he? I'd call that rude."

"Well," Grandma Holmes said with a smile, "sometimes I massacre a chicken and we all eat it fried. I've even heard of boys and girls eating hamburgers and hot dogs, which don't just grow on trees, you know."

Bob saw the point, but it did not ease his concern for Kip's safety. The hunter could collect a bounty on Kip, whether or not he was a pet. If the man spotted Kip at some distance from the ranch house, his dogs would run the young coyote down and kill him before they could be stopped.

Grandma Holmes sensed the belligerence swelling inside Bob. "You let your grandfather do any talking that needs to be done," she told him. "He knows how to deal with folks."

"All right, Grandma," Bob said as he hurried after his grandfather to hear what might be afoot.

The customary small talk about the day's weather and other subjects of little consequence was over by the time Bob stopped by the pickup. Pretending interest in the greyhounds milling around behind the slats that held them, Bob listened to the two men, who were standing at the truck's front.

"How's the coyote situation up here now?" Mr. Parker asked. "Heard many lately?"

"A man can always hear them up here," Grandpa said. "A body could never tell how many are around from just listening to them howl, though, I reckon."

Mr. Parker nodded idly as he pulled a dry grass stalk from the yard and began chewing on it.

"Awful dry through this part of the state this summer," he commented. "My dogs have run more than one coyote lately by the sight of the dust it raises."

"Yep," Grandpa said. "It's a shame when things get that dry. Some folk've got to saying that the run-down coyote population has something to do with it being so dry."

Mr. Parker laughed. "Yeah, I've heard some of that talk. I think some do-gooder or coyote-lover has sold folks a tall tale. You can't tell me a thieving coyote's got anything to do with the way it rains."

"No, it doesn't. But I've lived here some few years, and it rains as much now as it ever did. We just don't have the same water. If my corn had roots twenty feet long, it might get to the water table in the bottomland. The trouble, of course, is that the ground hasn't got enough grass cover the way it used to have."

"Yeah, that's what a fellow at the stock association was telling me." Mr. Parker leaned over the truck hood to blow a little cloud of dust from it. "The stock association's getting some of these schoolboy ideas, too. They tell me I'm the only coyote hunter they got a need for now."

"You must do all right then, with no competition," Grandpa said, not really asking a question, but meaning one.

"Well, not anymore. Coyotes are so scarce I barely kill enough to meet truck and dog food expenses, and I've been having to work the dogs hard for every scrawny one of them sheep killers."

Mr. Parker climbed back behind the steering wheel of his truck. "You care if I let the dogs scout around for coyote dens on your property here?" he asked.

"Well, I'd rather you wouldn't," answered Grandpa. "I'd kind of like to leave any coyote around here alone. My grandchildren are out visiting, and they've got a coyote pup for a pet."

"I see. Well, I wouldn't want to take a pet."

"You're welcome to drive your truck on through anytime you've a notion to, though. You're sure you won't stay for a bite of breakfast?"

"I'm much obliged to you, anyway, but I'd better be getting along. I'll wind up shearing sheep for a living if I don't get a move on."

Grandpa nodded. "You might keep an eye out for those clouds I see every few days over the mountains. Some of the dry washes can change real quick with a flash flood rolling down them."

"I don't doubt it," Mr. Parker called as he drove off the way he had come.

"Grandpa, you don't suppose he'll happen across Kip, do you?" Bob asked as they walked back toward the house.

"No," Grandpa assured him. "As long as Kip stays close around the house here with you two watching him like a mama coyote, I'd say he's about as safe as a coyote could be."

The dust in the front yard was soft in places. It swirled up around Bob's shoes almost every time he set his foot down.

"Do you really think that a lot of coyotes

would keep the ground from being so dry?" he asked.

"Well, it'd be a step in the right direction. Nothing's really simple when it comes to balancing land and the life on it. Coyotes have a lot to do with it. Foxes and snakes and hawks help hold down the rats that eat all the grass seeds, too."

Grandpa pointed to the cornfield near the creek. The cornstalks were dried and wrinkled although still green.

"The Navahos get around the disadvantage of a dry field partly by planting a dozen or so kernels in each hole. When the corn comes up, each stalk helps shade those around it, but the corn still doesn't amount to much. You could never raise enough to fatten beef cattle that way."

"I don't see how anything can grow where it's as dry as it is here," Bob said, kicking up the dust.

"Most things can't. Each plant that does stay healthy here has got its own secret. Each one grabs what moisture it can and ignores the dry weather."

"How can it do that?"

"Well, take this juniper tree here," Grandpa said as he pulled a twig from a scraggly Utah juniper near the porch. "Instead of big soft leaves, it's got skinny needles that are covered with little scales like shingles on a roof."

"What good does that do?"

"Cuts down sweating."

"Sweating?"

"Yes. Plants lose a lot of water by evaporation. If you moved a cottonwood poplar away from the creek and put it up there on the mesa, it'd dry up in a day's time. Its leaves would lose all their water. But these skinny little juniper needles with their scales hold the water in."

Grandpa stepped over to a little pinyon pine near the house. "This does pretty much the same thing," he said, pulling off a pine needle. "Look how shiny it is. That's a kind of waterproof varnish that does the same thing as the juniper's scales."

Bob studied the pine needles. "How about that?" he said to himself. "I never knew that."

Grandpa picked up a rock and tossed it toward some prickly pear cactus. Bob looked over at the spiny plants.

"That cactus has waxy skin to waterproof it," said Grandpa, "and an inside like a sponge to store water."

He then pointed to a plant a few steps away. It looked like a small sunflower.

"Get one of those leaves, Bob, and I'll show you another trick."

Bob got one and handed it to him.

"You see how hairy this leaf is?" Grandpa showed Bob the stiff fuzz on the leaf surface. "This hair's like a blanket. It holds the air in place and forms a kind of insulation so that evaporation is slowed down. If it wasn't for that insulation, a hot wind would dry up the plant right quick."

"You'd make a dandy schoolteacher, Grandpa," Bob said in admiration. "You know so much."

"Now, how about that?" Grandpa said with a chuckle. "A person's bound to pick up a lot of information about what's around him if he keeps his eyes open — and lives as long as I have."

As they walked on, he commented, "There's one more set of plants with a smart trick when it comes to drinking." He pointed to a slope in the distance that was well sprinkled with sagebrush. All the bushes seemed to have been planted according to a pattern. None grew close to a neighboring plant.

"Each sagebrush clump out there has a big bunch of roots to drink up all the water near it every time it rains. Each bush keeps the other ones at a distance by filling the ground around it with its own roots."

Now Bob heard the sound of footsteps around

the house corner. Marie burst into sight, breath-less from running.

"Is he gone?" she gasped.

Bob nodded and pointed toward the dust raised by the hunter's disappearing truck. "Where's Kip?" he asked.

"I don't know," she answered, still breathing hard. "I saw him out in the cantaloupe patch a few minutes ago. But before I could make him hear me, he took out after a rabbit."

"You mean he's gone?"

"He sure is!"

15

$\mathbb{B}$ob and Marie spent the rest of the morning searching for Kip. They ranged in ever wider sweeps of the area where Marie had seen him disappear after the rabbit. They called him by name, which should have brought him running as it always had before. By noontime, they had searched up canyon for nearly a mile, well past the point where the creek began as seepage from beneath a boulder.

"We'd better go on back and eat lunch," Bob finally told Marie. Both of them were tired, and her legs were scratched in a dozen places by the brush they had climbed through.

"I wouldn't worry too much about Kip," Grandpa said as they ate. "A coyote is even smarter than a dog in many ways, and any kind of a dog would never get lost in country like this."

Grandpa's words held little comfort for Bob, however. What worried him was the likelihood of the bounty hunter's greyhounds picking up Kip's trail and running him down. Kip didn't stand a chance of outdistancing such tough, lean dogs bred for speed and coyote killing.

"We want to look around some up on the mesa after lunch," Bob said. "Kip ought to see us or hear us if we call from some high place."

"Yes, he probably will," Grandpa said. "I want you two back right soon, though, if those clouds up to the north there get any darker. It's been a long time since we've had a hard rain here this time of summer, but it has happened and could happen again. If it does start raining all of a sudden, don't get under an overhang in a gully anywhere; get up on a slope."

"We'll run back, Grandpa, if it even looks like it might rain," Marie assured him.

Bob guessed that Grandpa was not entirely

convinced of the wisdom of allowing them out this afternoon. Consequently, he was much relieved when he and Marie made it out of calling distance without being called back.

After the hot climb to the mesa rim, Bob could see what bothered Grandpa. The sky over the San Francisco Peaks north of Flagstaff was dark. Off to the northeast, on the Navaho Reservation, slanting sheets of rain connected the low clouds and the desert.

"We'd better not waste much time," Bob said as they paused to catch their breath. "Kip might crawl in a hole in a gully to get out of the rain and get drowned."

During the next half hour, they moved from high place to high place, pausing on each for several minutes to cup their hands to their mouths and call, "Here, Kip! Here, Kip!"

There was no sign of Kip — nor of the bounty hunter. Bob could take little satisfaction in not seeing the man, however. Kip could very well be dangerously near him and his dogs, wherever that might be.

The sultry air of early afternoon was beginning to change. Bob could feel occasional fresh puffs of a cooling breeze upon his face. He studied the rainstorms off to the north. They were much closer than when he had last looked at them. He fancied he could even smell rain.

"We'd better start back, Marie," he said. "We've stayed out too long already."

"Couldn't we look just a little longer?" she pleaded. "We might find Kip just over the next hill. If we leave him, he might never come back."

"You know what we told Grandpa," Bob argued. "He might stop us from coming out by ourselves at all if we don't mind him."

Marie nodded her head in agreement and fell in behind him. They were still a hundred yards from the rimrock when they heard the first raindrops splattering behind. In the next few seconds, the rain swept over them. They were soaked by the time they got to the rim and found a rock shelf that offered some protection.

"Grandpa's going to skin us," Marie said as they shivered in their soaked clothes.

"He's going to be mad, that's for sure. He may not let us out of the yard from now on."

Through the gray curtain of rain, Bob could just make out the ranch house in the canyon below. Both Grandpa and Grandma Holmes were standing on the back porch looking toward the rimrock. Finally Bob distinguished a pair of binoculars before Grandpa's eyes.

"Let's both wave so they'll know we're all right," Bob said.

They stood and waved vigorously. After a moment, Grandpa waved back; then he and

Grandma Holmes walked back into the kitchen.

Bob and Marie watched the trickle in a nearby gully swell into a muddy stream, which washed the rock shelves clean of accumulated dirt. Soon the silt-filled water carried with it clumps of grass and brush. Occasionally small rocks were dislodged and rolled with the current, breaking loose larger rocks when they brushed against them.

"Look at that!" Bob exclaimed, pointing to the destructive process of the water rushing before them. "A few years of that could really dig out a ditch. I bet that's just the way Grand Canyon got started."

Below, Bob could see the rain-swollen creek. It was already out of its banks and swirling over land that had been so dry an hour ago that it would grow nothing but cactus and desert plants. Now the water was scouring it clean of loose soil, for there was no grass down there to slow the water and give it time to soak into the ground. The surrounding slopes and the mesa were naked except for twisted junipers and pinyons. There was no grass there to act as a sponge and soak up the rain.

The creek was a boiling millrace now. Downstream, the current dug a huge cottonwood poplar's roots free of the bank. The tree began falling, slowly at first, then faster as all support gave way. It made a tremendous splash.

Marie gripped Bob's elbow. "Did you see that?" she asked.

Bob nodded. "I'm glad we weren't down there trying to use that for shelter."

The rainstorm swept on toward the south after a few minutes. In a short time, the sun was out and heating the ground. Gentle steam rose from every rock crack and sand area into which rainwater had seeped. By the time Bob and Marie had climbed down the slope to the creek, there were dry spots on the ground, and even a few dust spots in highly porous soil.

The creek was already subsiding, and they quickly found a rock-strewn area where they could cross safely. Grandpa met them on the back porch. To Bob's relief, he did not seem to be mad.

"That's one way to learn when to get in out of the rain," he grunted, helping them out of their muddy shoes. "I think you two will start back a little earlier next time, won't you?"

"You bet." Bob nodded and grinned as he shivered in his wet clothes.

"You didn't find any trace of the pup?"

"No," Marie said. Her face was drawn. Bob knew she was on the verge of crying. As she started into the house, her toe stubbed the doorsill, and she fell against the screen. One hand went through the lower part of the rusty screen wire. That touched off her crying, which was as uncontrolled as the flash flood had been a few minutes ago.

Grandma Holmes quickly caught Marie up into her lap. "Now, now," she said soothingly. "Kip's probably out chasing another rabbit." She smiled. "Or maybe one of those big black-tailed jackrabbits is chasing him."

"But that bounty hunter may kill Kip!" Marie wailed as she turned her face into her grand-mother's neck.

"Well, after seeing the surprise Kip gave that rooster one day, I think he's smart enough to take care of himself."

Bob did not remember just what awakened him so early the next morning. His eyes opened slowly, and his mind shed sleep reluctantly. The first thing that caught his eye was his sister across the room.

She was still sound asleep. She must be cold, Bob decided, for her knees were drawn up against her chest, and her arms were wrapped around her legs. But what made her look so peculiar was the fact that she looked so comfortable lying on the hard floor. She even seemed to be smiling.

Bob twisted himself to a sitting position and slid his feet to the floor. He would have to wake her up and get her back into bed before she caught a cold.

He climbed wearily to his feet and shuffled over to Marie. As he bent to shake her shoulder, he noticed the blanket on her bed move slightly. Two pup feet stretched out from the blanket's edge. His eyes open wide now, Bob reached up and drew back the cover.

A yawning mouth — Kip's — greeted him. All the pup's tiny white teeth showed plainly as his tongue curled out in pleased comfort. Kip slowly closed his mouth and quietly licked his lips, as he rolled to his stomach and slid his chin between his forefeet.

Then, ever so slowly, he lifted one eyelid. Seeing Bob, he closed it quickly.

16

Bob touched Marie's shoulder to awaken her. Her eyes opened slowly. When she realized she had fallen off her bed, a look of consternation crossed her face.

Bob pointed to the lump under her blanket. As Marie climbed to the bed and slipped her feet under the warm cover, she still seemed unaware of what Bob meant. Suddenly she sat erect.

"Say," she began, but words left her, and

she lifted the cover to see Kip's wet nose on her stomach. "Kip!" she yelped happily. Pulling him against her chest, she hugged him tight. While Kip licked her neck and cheek, she slid to her pillow.

Curious about the commotion, Grandma Holmes stepped in from the kitchen. Seeing Kip's bobbing head, she smiled.

"Well, look who's here," she said, walking toward Marie's bed.

She patted Kip on the head. He eyed her suspiciously, waiting to see if he would soon be on his way out. But Grandma Holmes made no effort to evict him this time.

"I wondered what pushed open that ripped place you made in the screen door, Marie," Grandma said. "Come to think of it, there was some mud on the kitchen floor, too."

"Where's Grandpa?" Bob asked.

"Oh, he went up the canyon a while ago to hunt Kip."

They were halfway through breakfast before Grandpa returned.

"I couldn't find the young rascal anywhere," he said as he entered the kitchen. "I'll look some more after breakfast."

They managed to keep straight faces as Grandpa pulled his chair up to the table. Kip was in Marie's lap, and Grandpa had not seen him yet. A moment passed; then two pointed ears popped into sight behind Marie's plate. Grandpa stared in amazement, his forkful of pancake stopped before his open mouth. Finally he stuck the fork into his mouth and continued eating.

"Of all the nerve," he muttered, frowning at Kip in mock anger. "I hope some old pack rat carries you off for good sometime."

During the day, Bob noticed that Marie seemed to be absorbed in thought. Her attention was fully occupied by Kip, and she kept trying to pick him up. In late afternoon, Bob noticed that the coyote pup was limping.

"What's the matter with Kip?" he asked.

"He scratched his leg on a thorn bush, I think. It's beginning to swell up," Marie explained.

Lifting Kip to his lap, Bob examined the pup's swollen foreleg. The leg was sensitive, and Kip was touchy about it. The scratch was small, no longer than a half inch, but it was obviously infected.

"We'd better get Grandpa to look at it," Bob said. "Kip might have blood poisoning or something."

Grandpa sat down on the back step and turned Kip stomach up upon his knees while he studied the leg. Kip showed little confidence in the results of such treatment and kept trying to soothe his leg with his tongue.

"It's infected all right," Grandpa said. "We'll try some saltwater soaking first. If that does no good, we may take him into town to a veterinarian."

"Why'd it get infected?" Marie asked. "I saw Kip lick it good and clean."

"That's probably what did it," Grandpa said. "Most all animals try to soothe their hurts with their tongues, the way people do if they get stung by a bee. It's just natural to use something cool and moist. I've even watched animals wallow around in mud when they've gotten cut or hurt."

"But Kip didn't get his leg muddy. He kept it clean with his tongue."

"That's just the trouble, Marie. If you took a microscope and looked at some of the saliva on Kip's tongue, you'd see all sorts of germs and bacteria. That's what caused the infection."

"But, Grandpa, he's as clean as we are."

"Well, almost. If you were to take some human saliva and look at it, you'd find quite a bit of bacteria there, too. The veterinarian showed me this under his microscope one day when I was over at his place with a sick calf."

As Grandpa poured hot water into a pan and added a handful of salt, he explained more. "The food that people and animals eat gets stuck around their teeth, and the bacteria lives off it. The reason dogs and coyotes and other animals have many more germs than people is that they can't brush their teeth. Besides, they're apt to eat almost anything they find."

"Grandpa," Marie said, "you act as if it's wrong for a puppy to kiss someone."

Grandpa smiled wryly while he held Kip's swollen foot in the warm salt water. "There sure is. It's like taking a paintbrush full of germs and painting them across a little girl's hand or face. Anywhere there's a little nick in the skin, those germs fall in and get to work."

Sobered by this new idea, Marie and Bob viewed Kip in a new light as they took turns holding him in his antiseptic bath during the next half hour.

"We'll do this about every two hours," Grandpa said. "If the swelling gets any bigger by morning, I'll take Kip into town."

Luckily, the swelling was down by morning.

Bob wondered if Kip noticed the slight change in his and Marie's methods of play over the next few days. They played as much — petting him, smoothing back his hair, playing tag, and wrestling — but they carefully kept the pup's tongue off their hands and faces. Bob finally decided that Kip really didn't notice the difference. He was the same happy, rollicking pup.

Grandpa taught Bob and Marie much about pup care. He showed them how to comb seeds from Kip's fur. There were thousands of these because many weeds, and such plants as needle-and-thread grass, had seeds that were readily picked up by the soft hair. They also learned to search Kip's ears and other tender skin for ticks that set up temporary homes there. Bob made the ticks drop off by touching them each with a drop of iodine.

A few nights later, both Bob and Marie lay awake long after bedtime. They talked across the darkened bedroom.

"What do you suppose is going to happen to Kip after we go back home?" Marie asked. "He probably won't live in his box on the porch when he's grown."

"I don't know," Bob said. "I guess he'll find himself a female coyote this fall, and they'll have a family. Then when we come back sometime, maybe Kip will let us see his pups."

"Say, wouldn't that be nice!" Marie paused for a moment, thinking. "But he may never find a female coyote. I bet that bounty hunter's killed every one for miles. I don't remember hearing any coyotes howling at night lately."

Bob realized with a shock that recent nights had been free of coyote songs. Maybe that bounty hunter really had systematically shot or poisoned every single coyote. And, even worse, when Kip began roaming the mesa like any wild coyote, probably sooner or later the hunter would spot him and send his greyhounds after him. The thought was appalling.

Twice during the next week, as Bob and Marie hiked along the rimrock with Kip ranging out from their path, they saw the bounty hunter's pickup truck in the distance. With the coyotes so scarce and the man's income severely reduced because of it, he was combing the mesa and canyons thoroughly. No coyote could escape detection for very long.

"I've been wondering," Marie said one afternoon, as she and Bob headed back toward the ranch house after hunting horned lizards on the mesa. "Do you suppose Kip'll know how to live like a wild coyote when he's grown up?"

"I don't know," Bob answered. "He's gotten used to our getting food for him. He might not be smart enough to catch his own when small animals get scarce this winter."

Bob's worry about this was soon eased, however. As they walked along the rimrock toward the gully that let them climb down to the slope below, they saw Kip trotting on a parallel path below them. Apparently he had found a crack in the rimrock and climbed down to explore the slope. As they watched, he suddenly yelped and began loping in a circle around a bush.

"What's gotten into him?" Marie asked.

Hurrying to a point directly above Kip, Bob and Marie dropped to their hands and knees and stared over the cliff.

"There's a porcupine down there!" Bob exclaimed. "Kip will get himself into sure-enough trouble now."

Calling frantically, both children tried to make Kip let the porcupine alone. But Kip was too absorbed in his feud to leave the animal. The pain of quills in his nose had left no lasting impression on Kip, Bob thought in disgust as he watched the two.

The porcupine was not close to a tree, and so could not escape Kip's harassment. Kip romped around it, staying beyond reach of its lashing tail, but snapping at its face. He seemed to take an endless satisfaction in this strange sport. He was in no hurry and moved just fast enough to keep the harassed porcupine twisting and turning. Several times the porcupine tried to make a break for a tree, but Kip barred its path and kept it turning.

As minutes passed, the porcupine grew more indignant and made short lunges at Kip. This seemed to have no effect on the circling Kip. He simply continued the maddening game. Finally the angry porcupine had its fill of this treatment. It stood on its hind feet, instinctively trying to get into a position to close with its tormentor and end the fight.

At that moment, Kip proved his suitability for adult life in the wild. He darted in, his jaws tearing at the porcupine's unprotected stomach. Before the animal could bring a single quill between itself and the coyote, it died.

"Wow!" Bob exclaimed. "Did you see that?"

Marie nodded in awe at their pet's demonstration of wildlife wisdom. "Who'd ever guess little Kip could do that?"

When Grandpa heard their excited story a half hour later, he said, "Well, that's good. I've heard of coyotes using that trick before, but I wouldn't have guessed that young rascal would have pulled it off without a mama coyote showing him how first."

Grandpa grinned and patted the triumphant Kip on his head. "Yes-siree," he said, "it looks as if you might be able to earn your own living this winter without having to take dinner with us every day."

17

A week after the rainstorm, the desertlike areas of the canyon and the mesa above were covered with delicate flowering plants, which seemed to have sprung magically from the rocks themselves.

"This is what it's like after a wet spring," Grandma Holmes explained to Bob and Marie as she surveyed the colorful scene from the ranch yard. "We usually don't see all of this so late in the summer. But no matter when we get our rain, we've got a jillion flower seeds lying in the dry sand and rock cracks, just itching to sprout and grow."

"How long will they last?" Marie asked.

"Only a few more days. They'll go to seed quickly now that it's dry, and we won't see most of them again until next spring."

Everywhere the two children roved over the next few days, Marie gathered up armfuls of orange Arizona poppies as she passed through them. They were not real poppies, Bob read in one of Grandma Holmes's flower books. They were related to greasewood, but that made no difference. Their five-petaled flowers were as showy as any poppy.

On the lower slopes were scattered stalks several feet high, topped with pink flower clusters. These were bee plants. It was easy to see how the plants got their name, for countless bees were busily extracting nectar from them. Bob even counted four hummingbirds doing the same.

Sometimes the children saw yellow spider-flowers, shaped like the pink bee plant's blossoms. Altitude, more than anything else, decided which plant grew where. The yellow spiderflower seldom strayed up slopes a mile above sea level, while the pink bee plant grew on the highest and coolest slopes in this part of the country.

These pleasure-filled days passed much faster than the first days at the ranch. In another two weeks, Bob and Marie would be on their way home. Bob tried to forget about having to leave, but he could not.

The main thing that bothered him was that there would be no one around this fall to watch over Kip. Grandpa and Grandma Holmes could not follow Kip around as he and Marie had done all summer. They had work to do.

Sooner or later, the bounty hunter would catch Kip, for every day the growing coyote ranged farther and farther from the ranch yard sanctuary. Twice during the final week of vacation, Bob stepped to the back porch as soon as he got up, only to find Kip gone. The coyote trotted back into the yard an hour or so later, his tongue lolling out from a chase after a rabbit or some other fleet-footed animal.

Kip's muscles were hard now. He had shed completely the awkwardness that had characterized his actions a short time ago. Although he was still the happy pet, he was beginning to acquire the reserve of an adult, like a dog leaving puppyhood behind. Bob was glad to see Kip rapidly reaching a point where he could take care of himself.

"I wish we had a few dozen of Kip's kinfolks in these canyons around here," Grandpa remarked to Bob one evening as they watched Kip stalk a rat near the barn. After a patient wait, Kip raced in to seize the scurrying rodent. "There's no telling how much money a fellow like me has to put out for cow feed, which I could be raising right here. And all because we can't use the water that we get the same as we always did."

"It's too bad something doesn't happen to put that bounty hunter out of business," Bob said.

Grandpa nodded. "Yep. If I had a family of coyotes living up there on the slope, and they knew no one would bother them, I bet the rats here would get mighty lonesome for company."

The next morning, Bob saw the bounty hunter's truck pass the front gate again. The man was heading toward the mesa by a back road.

"Anyone seen Kip this morning?" Bob called into the kitchen.

"No," Grandpa answered. "He's probably out on the mesa. I saw him headed up there an hour ago. And say, I think I saw another young coyote sitting up there on the rim."

Bob hastily explained about the hunter, and Grandpa gave permission for him and Marie to go find Kip immediately. Grandma Holmes packed them a paper sack full of sausage sandwiches, dropping in two apples for dessert. Then she gave them each a glass of milk to drink as a prerequisite for leaving.

"Do you suppose that other coyote could have been a female?" Marie asked between gulps of milk.

"I'd like to think so," Grandpa said, "but nobody could tell from this distance." He handed Bob his binoculars. "Be careful with these."

Bob and Marie were atop the rimrock in fifteen minutes. Glancing about, Bob looked for a rise in the ground that would give them the best observation point.

"Over there," he told Marie. "We'll look around from that little hill. With the binoculars, we ought to spot Kip before long."

Standing atop the hill, Bob held the binoculars to his eyes. He swept the horizon carefully, then scanned the foreground. He saw nothing moving, not even the hunter's pickup truck.

"See anything?" Marie asked impatiently.

"Not yet." Bob began a more systematic search of the rolling ground that made up the mesa top.

Marie touched his shoulder. "I see something moving out there toward the north." She pointed toward a scarcely perceptible movement on a slope. Aiming his binoculars toward the movement, Bob studied the area for a moment.

"You're right," he said. "It looks like Kip

all right, playing in some sagebrush. There seems to be some other animal with him.''

"Let me see,'' Marie said.

Bob handed her the binoculars. Her sharp eyes soon identified the second animal.

"It's another coyote,'' she exclaimed. "I guess it's the one Grandpa thought he saw this morning up here.'' She kept her eyes glued to the eyepiece. "Do you suppose it really is a female?''

"I hope so,'' said Bob. Suddenly, spotting a puff of dust to the west, he reached for the binoculars. "Let me have them, quick! I think that's the bounty hunter.''

Marie wasted no time giving the glasses to him. It took only a moment to check the dust cloud.

"It's him all right,'' said Bob. "He's on top of a ridge. He hasn't spotted Kip yet.''

"How far is Kip from him?''

"Half a mile, maybe. It won't take him long to find Kip once he starts looking over the countryside with his binoculars.''

Shortly Bob watched the pickup truck roll to a stop. Holding his binoculars steady, he saw the hunter get out and climb to the truck's front bumper. The man had binoculars in his hand, too, and he twisted slowly about to survey in all directions.

After a moment, Bob saw Mr. Parker's face turned in his direction and realized with embarrassment that the man was staring at him and Marie. Bob took his binoculars away from his eyes to get rid of the feeling that he had been caught peeking. Then he realized that this was ridiculous. He had as much right to stare as the bounty hunter had.

After focusing again upon the hunter, Bob guessed that he had discovered the two coyotes. The man's gaze was steady now as he studied the animals.

"He's trying to figure out a way to get close enough for his greyhounds to see them. Then he'll let his dogs out," Bob said.

The man soon climbed back into his pickup. The truck began rolling slowly, as if the man had not started the engine. Apparently he had just let it out of gear so it would coast out of sight.

Bob and Marie waited a full five minutes before getting a clue to the hunter's whereabouts. Then two buzzards flapped into the air in the distance, apparently startled from their feeding on a dead animal by the hunter's truck. Keeping his glasses on the area, Bob saw the truck move slowly into sight from behind a ridge.

The hunter got out and walked to an observation point. It took him only a moment to learn the position of the still unsuspecting coyotes. Then he went back to the truck and opened the tail gate. The greyhound pack spilled out of the truck like water from a hose. With a wave of his arm, the man showed the dogs the direction, and they were off in long graceful leaps.

Apparently they made no noise to alert the two coyotes. They were only two hundred yards from Kip when he finally lifted his head to listen.

"Oh," Marie groaned. "Why don't they run?"

"Kip's watching the dogs now," Bob reported hastily. "Now the other coyote's looking, too. There they go!"

"They can't outrun those dogs. Oh, Bob, we've got to do something. We can't just stand here!"

"There's nothing we can do. Kip can't hear us, and we sure can't head the dogs off."

Kip and his companion had disappeared from sight. Bob hoped they were racing along some secret pathway known only to them. He knew this was unlikely, though. The greyhounds probably knew this mesa better than the young coyotes, for they had hunted here several times.

"If they could only get into some thick brush, they could get away," Bob said, twisting his shoulder away from Marie's grip. She was unconsciously digging her nails into his muscles.

He handed the binoculars to her to ease her excitement. She pressed them to her eyes and swung them back and forth in a futile effort to find Kip. The dogs were out of sight now. Bob could see that much without the binoculars.

He looked at the hunter. The man was waiting at the point where the pursuit had begun. Bob guessed he was waiting to see in what direction the race headed before moving his truck again.

"I see them!" Marie screamed.

Bob looked toward the area where her binoculars were aimed. He saw the two dots that were Kip and his companion. Only a few bounds behind were the half dozen greyhounds, steadily closing the space between them and the coyotes.

In the animals' pathway were scattered clumps of agave, or century plants, each looking like a giant rosette of leafy daggers. Kip was using these to advantage, dodging among them and the scattered blackbrush. He seemed to be headed away from the rim, toward a forest of scraggly cedar, which hugged the reddish sand slopes a half mile to the north.

Only the vegetation saved Kip from immediate disaster. Stealing a glance toward the hunter, Bob saw the truck moving now. The man had joined the pursuit. If necessary, he could stop on a rise and wait with raised rifle. Then the next time Kip raced across an open area, he would stop a bullet and go down in a little cloud of dust as the dogs swarmed over him.

"Will he make it?" Bob asked.

"No, he won't," Marie said angrily. "Some of the hounds are going to cut Kip off."

Bob's gaze followed her pointing finger. Now he could see what she meant. A swirl of dust was moving slowly toward a point that would intercept the desperate young coyotes. These veteran greyhounds knew their business.

They're turning!" Marie exclaimed shortly. "Kip's turning back toward us."

She handed the binoculars back to Bob. Quickly he spotted the fleeing coyotes, whose bushy tails stood straight out behind them. One big white greyhound surged ahead of its companions, eager to end the chase. It drew abreast of Kip. Bob thought Kip did not see it, but suddenly the speedy young coyote darted aside, just a moment before reaching a group of century plants.

The greyhound was not able to turn as quickly. It turned a fraction of a second too late to avoid the studded plants. Bob held the binoculars on the unfortunate dog long enough to see it limp out of the dangerous plants.

Kip led the pursuit back toward the rimrock now. He took advantage of every piece of rough ground that would prevent the greyhounds' long legs from stretching out in full stride.

Bob saw that the hunter had also seen Kip's change in direction. He was driving faster across the rolling mesa on a bearing that would soon bring him near Kip's path. He would get a chance to make a close shot.

"Bob," Marie wailed again, "can't we do something?"

"It's up to Kip."

Bob saw Kip glance aside at the approaching pickup. The dogs were only a few feet behind him now.

Between Kip and the truck there was a boulder-strewn area leading toward the mesa rim. Kip turned brazenly toward it, heading directly at the pickup. This tactic seemed to puzzle the hunter. He stopped the truck and jumped out, bringing his rifle to his shoulder. He could not shoot, however, for fear of hitting his dogs, so close behind the two coyotes.

Another few feet put Kip into the rocky area, and he led his companion in a dodging, skillful race between the boulders. The hunter jumped back into his truck and accelerated after the racing animals, following a route parallel to the rocky area. In no time, the truck was even with Kip, and Bob could see the man attempting to aim his rifle out the window with one hand while he drove with the other.

Bob never knew whether Kip made his next maneuver on purpose, or whether he just had to do it in order to follow the roughest ground. In any event, Kip again turned toward the moving truck, with the dogs so close behind that they had started reaching for coyote heels.

Upon seeing his valuable dog pack about to be run down by his own truck, the hunter jerked the pickup aside. It was his undoing. One front wheel struck a boulder, and the door on the driver's side swung open. Mr. Parker was thrown out, but fortunately landed in thick brush. With no driver, the speeding truck swerved out of control. One of the front wheels caught another boulder, and the truck spilled on its side as dog pen slats flew in all directions.

Through the dust, a shower of sparks flashed as the metal truck scraped rock. Suddenly a ball of flame covered the truck's rear end. Apparently something had punctured the gas tank. The fire worked forward, and soon the whole truck was burning.

"My gosh!" Bob yelled as he jumped to his feet. "Let's go help."

He and Marie had taken only a few steps, however, when they saw Mr. Parker climb from the bushes where he had been thrown. He appeared unhurt. They slowed down.

"I guess there's nothing we can do," Bob said. "Let's just walk until we see if he wants help."

The hunter's dogs had lost Kip in the commotion, and already they were trotting back toward their master. The blazing truck and pillar of smoke boiling skyward held their attention.

"He's all right," Bob said, stopping. "He sure can't put out the fire now, and if we go down there, he might not be in the mood for company. Let's leave him alone. He'll come on down to Grandpa's after a while."

That made sense to Marie. She nodded.

To their delight, they found Kip waiting for them on the back porch. He looked a little bedraggled from the race, but it seemed to have had no effect on his appetite. He was busy eating a bowl of hot corn grits, which Grandma Holmes had set before him.

"Well," Grandpa said, "I see you found Kip." He chuckled as he looked at the group on the porch. His smile subsided quickly, however, when Bob told him what had happened.

"Are you sure he didn't get hurt?" Grandpa asked.

"I'm sure." Bob pointed back up to the rim. "That's him now just starting down here."

Grandpa took his binoculars and fixed them on the man. "He's carrying one of his dogs. He'll want me to take him into town pretty soon. Grandma, you fix him some coffee and hot biscuits, while I clean out the truck so I can haul his dogs."

He turned to Bob. "I think you'd better take Kip inside until we're gone. Those dogs won't know he's a pet."

As soon as Kip finished eating, Marie took him inside, while Bob helped his grandfather. Grandpa drove his pickup down to the creek to meet the tired hunter and bring him to the house.

Mr. Parker looked disgusted, Bob noticed, even after he had washed up and come into the kitchen.

"I'm sure much obliged to you folks for going to so much trouble," he told Grandma Holmes as she busied herself setting coffee and food before him.

Bob sat down at the table for a delayed breakfast. Marie soon joined them, having shut Kip in the bedroom.

"Is your truck ruined?" Grandma Holmes asked after Mr. Parker had had a few sips of coffee and a bite of biscuit.

Mr. Parker nodded. "It's not worth taking spare nuts off of now. It burned up as completely as if I'd built a fire under it. My rifle got burned up, too."

"That's bad," Grandma Holmes said sympathetically. "You sure did have a run of bad luck today."

"Well, it sure put me out of the coyote business real quick. I guess it'd take me five years to save up enough to get a rig fixed up like the one I had. By then, there'll be such a squawk about killing them coyotes that it wouldn't be worth the trouble."

The man shook his head. "What makes me feel so put out about it is that I was chasing a couple of the skinniest little old coyotes you ever did see."

Bob noticed that the bedroom door had swung ajar. He started to get up and close it, because he and Marie had not yet made up their beds. He decided not to, though. He might miss something.

"You should've seen that little old coyote in front," Mr. Parker told Grandpa as he hunched forward with both elbows on the table to finish his coffee. "That little mutt cut out of a pile of rocks straight toward me, and I had to yank the steering wheel to keep from killing my dogs. Before I knew it, I was watching my hunting rig go up in a cloud of smoke.''

He blew into his cup to cool the coffee. Bob's attention shifted to Marie. She was squirming around as if she were sitting on a tack. Then Bob saw the reason.

Kip had slipped out of the bedroom and was now at Marie's chair. He stood on his hind feet with his front paws in her lap, waiting for a handout. Marie didn't want to give him one with the hunter right there.

Kip tried a new tactic. He moved his front paws from Marie's lap to the table edge, then slid his long nose over the edge and between his paws. His pointed ears stood erect while he waited for someone to pass him some food.

Mr. Parker finished his coffee blowing. ''Yes, sir,'' he said, lifting the cup to his lips, ''if ever I get a chance . . .''

He failed to finish the sentence. His eyes widened and fixed on Kip across the table. Kip looked back in all innocence. But Bob saw an ever so slight expression on Kip's face. It sure looked like a grin.

Mr. Parker sat rigid and red-faced for another moment. Then he slowly put down his coffee cup and slid back his chair. ''Mighty fine — breakfast,'' he said on his way to the door.

Grandpa mercifully loaded him and his dogs quickly into the truck. In the next few minutes, they were heading toward town.

Bob and Marie's last night at the ranch was as memorable as their first one.

Bob slid his feet under the soft blankets with the same reluctance he might have felt about finishing a summer's last swim. This would be the last time he would bed down here for months to come. He and Marie probably would be back next summer, because Grandpa would write all the letters necessary to help wear down possible objections at home.

What was on his mind the most, however, was what was going to happen to Kip this fall and winter and spring. Marie seemed to be occupied with the same thoughts. She spoke across the bedroom.

"Do you suppose that coyote Kip was playing with will stay around here till Kip gets old enough to raise some pups?"

"I don't know. I guess coyotes like each other's company as much as people like each other. But Grandpa said coyotes don't really get interested in raising a family until about January every year."

"That other little coyote could travel to the West Coast by then," Marie said quietly.

"It sure could."

Bob clasped his hands behind his head as he lay back on his bed. He kept the cover down to his chest so he could enjoy better the treasured sounds and smells of the ranch.

A cricket chirped somewhere in the walls. A flying squirrel made a rustling sound on the roof over his bed. A poorwill sounded its mournful "poor-will, poor-will" from down canyon.

Bob sniffed, pretending he was a coyote sifting the night air for scent. The mustiness of creosote bush drifted off the mesa with the night breeze, as did the turpentine perfumes from pinyon pine resin. One strong odor identified a distant skunk or some bee plants crushed by cattle hoofs. Grandpa called them skunk plants. It was an appropriate name.

Bob was lying there without speaking when he heard a new sound on the night breeze. It seemed so natural that his thoughts did not grasp it until it faded. Then it began again from up on the rimrock.

It was a coyote howl. It began deep within the animal's chest and rose into an extended wail that quavered until it was two octaves higher. It was a song like no other song on earth, a song of the wild open spaces, a song that invited coyote feet to race the wind to the Painted Desert and back again.

Bob listened with waiting breath for another sound. There came the patter of Kip's paws on the back porch floor. Bob jumped up and ran to the kitchen window.

Kip was trotting to the brightest spot of moonlight in the backyard. He settled to his haunches and aimed his nose straight toward the Milky Way. His song began deep inside his chest, a low bark that rose higher and higher, climbing to the rimrock and past, to follow the night wind.

Bob smiled to himself. That was Marie's answer. Kip would be the head of a family next summer when they came back.